THE OCTOPUS ARM

G Logan

VISUALWORDING
USING WORDS TO PAINT A PICTURE

Copyright © 2020 G Logan.

ISBN: 978-1-7370676-1-0 (Paperback)
2nd Edition

Cover Art by Micheal Logan

Editing and Layout by Ellen Gehring

To request permissions, contact the publisher at
glogantheauthor@gmail.com

Printed by Lulu.com in the USA.

PRELUDE

"Lil C, wake up… We're home." Carl says to his son as he reaches into the backseat to shake his leg. "Come on now, you gotta get up or we're gonna leave you out here."

Little C hears his parents' doors open and quickly hops up. Halfway up the driveway, Lil C says… "Thank ya'll for taking me to the fair."

"You don't gotta thank us son. I'm sorry we don't have time to take you more places, but…" Carl pauses as he hears Lil C cutting him off.

"I know, I know. Somebody's gotta make the money so I can have nice things and enjoy my life. But what if I said I don't care about the nice things so much. I just like going places and doing things with ya'll."

Harriet is so touched by what Lil C just said that she makes a face like she's about to cry as she speaks. "Don't worry son. I promise we're gonna take the time to do all the things we want to do." Rubbing his head. "You talk like such a Lil man."

Unlocking the front door. "We need to check our dates again and make sure our son is thirteen and not thirty." Joked Carl.

Lil C giggles. "I'm only thirteen dad."

"Yeah I know" As they enter the house Carl notices the T.V. is on. "Honey, I thought you said you turned everything off when we left."

"I could've sworn I did," Harriet answered in a puzzled tone.

"I turned the T.V. on," Red said as he and Butch came out of the kitchen both holding nine-millimeter guns with silencers on them. (Red and Butch are drug runners for Carl and his partner Saint.)

As if he didn't care about his position. "What the fuck are ya'll doing in my house?"

Red lifted his gun directly in Carl's face. "Saint sent us to come talk to you and after sitting outside for over an hour, I figured it was in our best interest to let ourselves in to wait. You know how nosey your neighbors can be." Red displayed the most sinister grin.

"I swear to God you two gotta be out of your fuckin minds to come in my Muthafuckin…"

Red cracks Carl across the head with the but of his gun while shoving him to the couch before he could finish his sentence. "Shut the fuck up nigga before I splatter your ass permanently." Signaling to Harriet with his gun. "You get your little sexy ass over here on the couch next to your bloody husband." Staring at her seductively before he redirects his attention to Carl. "Now, what we came to talk to you about before you flipped out of control is the issue with you and Saint's partnership."

Spitting out blood before he speaks. "What the fuck you mean issue? I already told Saint he can have all control just give me mine, But if this is how he wants it to go down tell him I said I'm good and he can keep everything."

"He said you would probably say some shit like that. And he said he don't trust you as an enemy." Red's eyes looked full of murder as he grinds his teeth together.

"Well at least let my family go. This is between us." Carl said trying to hold his calm.

"Red started waving his gun in Carl and Harriet's face as he speaks. "You know we go way back, Carl. And I ain't got nothing but love for ya. But business is business and this is a job." Putting the barrel of his gun against Carl's forehead. "I'm gonna help you keep some of your dignity" Red pulled the trigger leaving Carl slumped on the couch next to his screaming wife. Pointing the gun at Harriet. "And for you baby. I got something special for you." Red strokes her thick thighs with his warm gun. Fighting through Harriet's kicking legs, Red rips her panties off from under her sundress. He rubs her womb with his fingers and sniffs them. "Oh, you do smell sweet."

Harriet trying to cover herself. "Please stop! Please stop!"

Red punched her in her face and climbed in her legs. He pumped her as hard as he could, ignoring her screams until he came inside her. Standing up fixing his pants Red massaged Harriet's face. "Now I see why Carl was always so protective of you. Shit, I don't wanna share that good pussy with nobody else either now that it's mine." Smiling a wink at her.

Harriet stood to her feet. "I will never be yours, you fucking bitch!" Harriet spits a glob in Red's face. "I hate you!"

"You stupid bitch!" Red wiped the spit from his eyes and shot Harriet in the head leaving her lifeless next to her husband. Turning his gun towards Butch who has been holding and gagging Lil C during this whole ordeal. "Finish the kid!"

Butch who hasn't said a word this entire time burst out. "This wasn't part of the plan! You're just going fuckin crazy! Butch pointed his gun at Red, leaning over Lil C as he shielded him with his body. "He's not ready for the octopus arm! (Which was his way of saying somebody wasn't ready for the death or danger that was coming to them.)

"Fuck your octopus arm!" Red shouted as he shot Butch in the chest, barely being missed by the shot that came out of Butches gun.

Butch fell with all his weight on top of Lil C and said in a faint voice. "I'm sorry nephew."

Red walked over to where Butch was covering Lil C and squatted down next to them poking the tip of his gun into Lil C's ribs. Pow!

CHAPTER 1

The air on the ICU floor is brisk, so Carol Jones, who is Carl's twin sister is snuggly bundled in a blanket as she watched her nephew lying unconscious in the bed. "How many tubes do they need?" Carol mumbled under her breath as she studies the many connections. (There is a tube in Lil C's nose, one in his mouth going down his throat, one in his left side, one in his right side, a catheter, a colostomy bag, and two IVs and all kinds of little wires connected to the pads for his heart monitor.) "Everythings going to be alright. You just hold on and keep fighting. Do you hear me? Keep fighting." Whispering in Lil C's ear Ms. Jones takes his hand. "I know you can hear me honey, but I'm going to need you to show everyone else you can hear me. Try to squeeze my hand." She thought she felt Lil C flinch but seeing him still lifeless she felt maybe she wanted him to wake up so bad, that she was imagining it. Seconds later he squeezed her hand again. Then again. "Doctor! Doctor! Get in here! He's moving!"

Lil C opened his eyes and looked up at his aunt who's face is soaked in tears.

"I'm here baby. Auntie's right here." Lifting her hand towards the sky. "Thank you, Jesus! Hallelujah! Thank you, Lord! You deserve praise!"

Within seconds a nurse came into the room. "Did he wake up?"

Ms. Jones spoke with excitement. "I told him to shake my hand and he did.... Like three or four times! Then when I started shouting he opened his eyes and looked at me! Oh my God, you are real." Ms. Jones took Lil C's hand again and said, "Ok baby, everyone's here to see you. Open your eyes. Seeing no response. "I know you're tired baby, but open your eyes one more time for auntie."

Lil C's eyes opened up slowly and stayed open for a few seconds before closing again.

"We've been waiting for you to wake up for three days now."
The nurse said in the sweetest voice, as she checked his vitals.
"He's still heavily medicated but when the Dr. gets in here he'll
probably drop his meds down some. So until then just expect him
to be in and out like this." Before walking out of the room the
nurse turns and hugs Ms. Jones. "I'm not supposed to do this, but
I am so happy for you right now. Your prayer worked." Giving
one last smile the nurse exits the room.

The next two weeks felt like forever. It seemed like every other
day the nurses would come in and unhook another life assisting
accessory until finally Lil C wasn't connected to anything. After
being in the hospital for a month he was released to go home with
his aunt.

The car ride home was totally silent until Lil C spoke. "Did my
parents have a big funeral?"

Well everybody in the whole city seemed to be there. The only
people I didn't see there were your dad's friends Saint and Red.
The funeral was probably too much for them to bear. Saint and
your dad have been friends since elementary school." Biting her
lip to hold back showing her emotions. "I know it's wrong to
wish bad on people, but I hope Saint and Red take care of
whoever killed my brother." Ms. Jones let out a gasp trying to
take in what she had said. "Look Lil C… I know you told the
detectives you didn't see anyone's face, but could you recognize
anyone's voice?"

"No, ma'am. It all just happened so fast" Lil C answered
looking out his window to hide his face.

"Well do you even remember how Uncle Butch got on top of
you?"

"He was tryna keep me from getting shot. He said he wouldn't
let the octopus arm kill me, then he got shot and fell on top of
me." Lil C continued looking out the window at the sky. "Do you
think we could stop by the cemetery on the way home? I just
want to see where my parents are buried."

9

"Are you sure you don't want to wait?" She asked, considering Lil C's health. "you know you can't be standing for extended periods of time."

"Yes, ma'am… I'm sure. I feel like I've waited too long already."

Tapping the tears from her eyes before they fully developed. "Well if your sure you're up to it I don't see any reason why we can't stop by." Making a right detouring her direction. "I know this has got to be hard on you." Ms. Jones says as she pulls into the cemetery. "Just know that if you want to turn around and leave at any time, all you have to do is say so."

"I will." Lil C said watching the headstones as they drove through the cemetery.

As she puts her car in park alongside the curvy road Ms. Jones suggests. "You know you don't have to go all the way up to it. I can just point to it from here."

"I need to do this. I never got to say goodbye. I just want to see them." Lil C's voice shook as he spoke.

They both exit the car. Ms. Jones puts her arm under Lil C's to support him as she guides him to the gravesite. "This is it, baby. This is where your parents are buried."

Noticing both his parents' names on one huge headstone Lil C asked his aunt "Are they buried on top of each other?"

"No Lil C. I got a coffin special made to fit both of them side by side so that they will always be together." Noticing Lil C turning his back and wiping his tears. "I'm going to wait in the car. I know you probably got some things you want to get off your chest that's between ya'll." Lil C began praying, but not to God, to his parents. "Mom, I know you told me that part of life is letting go, but this time you were wrong. I'm never gonna let go. I'm so sorry I couldn't help you. I was trying to get free." Losing his words as he lets out a cry. "Dad, you said there was going to be a day when you wouldn't be here no more, and I was going to have to be my own man… Well, you don't have to worry about me. I'm going to stay focused and I'm going to get Uncle Saint and Uncle Red back for what they did to ya'll… I love you guys, and I miss you so much. " Lil C's emotions started getting the best of him and he began to slump over weak as he cried.

Ms. Jones who is totally in tears as well walks back to her nephew and embraces him. "Everything's gonna be ok... Let's go to the house."

The ride to the house was just as quiet as the ride to the cemetery. The silence broke as soon as Ms. Jones pulled in her driveway. C! C! Ms. Jones son Xavier came running to the car. "Come in the house so I can show you my room. My mom said you're gonna share it with me cause you gonna be staying a whole lot of nights."

Smiling at the excitement his little cousin has. "Just give me a second. I gotta get out of the car first. What's been up with you though?"

"I've been good. My mom bought me a new fighting game. We can play, when you come in"

"Well go and make sure everything in the room is ready for me and hook the game up, so I can get straight to beating you." Lil C tries to mock Xavier's energy. Watching him run into the house Lil C says "I guess somebody was ready for me to come home."

"You couldn't imagine. He hasn't been asleep for the past two days since I told him you were coming here to stay. I'm surprised he gave in so easily and ran off."

"Yeah I better not keep him waiting." Looking serious. "Auntie... Do you think you could take me to my parent's house to get some stuff?"

Shaking her head. "Oh no honey. No one can go into the house until the police release it. Besides I don't know if that's the smartest place for you to be with your parents killer still out there running free."

CHAPTER 2

It's been five months since the shooting and Lil C is almost back to his healthy energetic self. Putting Xavier in a wrestling move. "Tap out! Tap out!"

Grunting trying to get loose. "Never!

Applying more pressure. "You gonna cry? You better tap out!"

Xavier Growling. "Never!"

Ms. Jones' voice stopped all the fun. "You two better stop wrestling in my living room before I tap both of you out." Holding up her fist.

Pushing Xavier away. "Get out of here you pain freak. I swear any other kid would've been tapped out."

Quickly getting back to his feet. "That's because I'm tougher than any other kid."

In total agreement "Yeah you're tougher than any other kid… but what about smarter?"

"I'm smarter too!" Xavier said in a cocky tone.

"Then whats six plus three?" Questioned C.

Quickly adding his fingers up. "Nine!"

"What's five plus eight?"

Taking a little longer than the first time. "Thirteen!"

"Alright, smarty pants… What's ten minus five?"

"That's easy.. That's five! I don't even need to use my fingers on that one," Xavier exclaimed, feeling his self.

"Well, I think you're doing great at learning your math." Ms. Jones interrupted. "Now go add up some soap and water and get yourself clean so we can have dinner."

'Yes, ma'am!" Xavier yells as he runs out of the living room to carry out his mother's task.

"C come let me talk to you real quick." Ms. Jones signaled for C to come sit next to her.

Sounding nervous. "Did I do something wrong?"

"No, you didn't do anything wrong. I wanted to talk to you about your mom and dad's house."

"What about it?"

The police are done with their investigation… Well, at least the part that they needed your parent's house for. So they have released the keys to me and I know you said you wanted to go get some stuff before. Did you still want to go or would you rather I go get your stuff for you?" Ms. Jones asked mindfully

Lil C answered quickly. "No… I wanna go. I just want to see the house."

"As soon as we finish dinner, we can go there together. I got a few things I have to check on over there anyway. Realizing she hasn't heard from Xavier for a few minutes she looks down the hall towards the bathroom. "Xavier are you alright?"

Yelling as loud as he could. "Yes, ma'am. I had to go to the bathroom."

"Well hurry up in there so your cousin can use the bathroom."

"Yes, ma'am!"

Bringing her attention back to Lil C. "Is everything ok?" Noticing him with his head down. "If you want to wait till later I understand."

Lifting his head. "No, I wanna go tonight. I was just thinking about how much I wish they were here."

"It's ok to miss them. It's just not ok to let that stop you from living. Speaking of them, have you been able to remember anything new? I know you're tired of me asking but the doctors said you can gain more memory as time goes by." Asking hopefully.

"No, ma'am." Looking down. "If I did remember who it was, would you hate me for wanting to kill them?"

Hugging Lil C. "Baby I could never hate you. But if you know something, I want you to tell me so I can have the police arrest whoever it is so we can all be safe."

Thinking to himself that jail wasn't a good enough punishment for the gruesome execution of his parents. "I really don't know. I was just asking because I don't know if I am right or wrong for wishing I knew so I could kill them myself." Looking more adamant than ever.

Lifting his chin to make him look her in the eyes. "I wouldn't say you were wrong to feel that way. That's just part of being human. I mean you think that I don't ever wish I had the power to avenge my brothers' death. We're twins for God's sake. We've never been apart and now someone took my brother from me. The truth is nephew, if I had a gun and your parens killer was right in front of me, I would probably make the unchristian like decision and pull the trigger. Maybe that's why God hasn't and hopefully won't put me in that situation because he knows I wouldn't be strong enough to fight off the demon of hate." Dropping a single tear.

"I'm done in the bathroom momma" Xavier came shouting back into the living room. He soon lost his excitement when he notices his mom's gloomy face. "What's the matter?" He asked with great concern.

Wiping her eyes dry and cracking a smile. "Everything's ok honey. We're just talking about your Uncle Carl and Aunt Harriet."

"I miss them a lot." Sounding so innocent. "I had a dream he came over and was giving me a big hug like before. And he hugged me so tight that I woke up."

Addressing Xavier's dream Lil C says. "That was probably his way of telling you bye." Giving a head gesture towards the kitchen. "Let's go in here so we can eat."

Shortly after dinner Ms. Jones, Lil C, and Xavier all went to Lil C's parents' home. As soon as they pulled in the driveway Ms. Jones says. "We're only going to be in here for about twenty minutes. So you don't have to be in a super rush, but you can't take all day either."

Lil C let out a sigh. "I can't believe last time I was here I lost my parents and almost got killed myself."

Xavier reassures Lil C. "I won't let nothing happen to you. If the bad guys come I'm gonna do my Dragon Ball moves and beat them up." Demonstrating a few strikes in the air.

Egging him on. "That's all I need to know. Can't nobody touch me as long as you got my back." Although the walk to the front door was short. It seemed to go in slow motion in Lil C's head as he remembered what had happened that night. He also thought to himself. What if Red was waiting for them right now? Watching his aunt put the key in the door, Lil C grabbed her hand. "Let me go first" As soon as he walked in he checked to make sure the TV was turned off. "Wait right here for a sec while I check around." Whispers C. He walked around nervously with the poker to the fireplace as he checked every closet and corner of the house. "It's cool to move around now. Everything's clear." The house was just as he last remembered it to be, minus the couch his parents died on.

"Lil C bring everything you want to take with you to the door and we'll pack it up all at once." A sad feeling took over as she notices a puddle of dried up blood on the floor.

Seeing what has caught her attention he points. "That's where I was laying. You would think they would've cleaned up all this blood when they were in here all this time."

"Is that your blood too?" Xavier asked pointing to where the couch used to be.

Immediately Lil C started crying. "No that's my mom and dad's blood." Gagging as to almost throw up. "I need to get that up"

"Don't worry about cleaning any of this. I'm going to clean all this up. You just go and get your stuff together. I think you have seen enough blood to last you a lifetime." Grabbing Xavier's arm. "You stay down here with me."

Lil C went through his room like a tornado throwing all his favorite clothes in a pile. Then as quietly as he could he tiptoed down the hall to his parents' room. Upon entering the room Lil C lifted the mattress. "Damn... The police must've taken it." Under his breath referring to his dad's gun that he knew was always there. Flopping on the bed crying in despair. "What am I suppose to do now?" Looking towards the ceiling as if his parents could hear him. "What would you do?" Then it hit him. "Ah... the gun from the takeover." Lil C ran hurriedly downstairs yelling. "I'll be right back up!" As he passed through the living room.

Watching her nephew running through Ms. Jones wiped her eyes and said a quick prayer. "Please Lord bless Lil C with the strength and endurance to make it through this with all his wits."

Lil C went under the stairs in the basement and removed a loose brick that easily slid out. He then reached in the hole and pulled out a towel with something wrapped inside. Immediately his mind drifted to the first time he saw this towel.

"Son, I'm about to show you something cool. But first, you gotta promise you won't tell anyone. And I mean anyone. Not even your mother." Carl said in a stern voice

"What is it?" Lil C asked anxiously

"Promise and I'll tell you," Carl said reiterating the deal.

Making a cross with his fingers over his chest. "I promise dad, now tell me."

Carl pulled a towel out of a hole in the wall and unwrapped it revealing a chrome nine-millimeter pistol with a pearl handle. It had gold trimmings and a silencer. It also had engraved in the side of the barrel, NO REMORSE. "This gun was used to take down the four druglords that used to run this city. Isn't she beautiful?" Marveling the artwork.

"Who took down the drug lords?" Lil C asked enchanted by his dad's story.

Well as the story goes... It was a young man with the heart of a lion, and the thirst for wealth like a vampire in a blood bank. It's said that he took them out one by one through the course of one night as they slept comfortably in their beds. Within a week this guy and one of his childhood friends took over everything, and that's why he got these words engraved in his gun." Rubbing the gun like a magic lamp.

"How did you get the gun dad? Did you know the guy?" Asked Lil C.

"Now that's a whole other story. I'll have to tell you when you get a little older." Wrapping the gun back up and returning it to its place in the wall.

C's mind came back to the present with him holding the towel that he quickly unfolded displaying the shiny chrome and gold of this legendary gun. Holding that gun in his hand, Lil C felt like he finally had the strength he had been looking for. The power to avenge his parents' death. He hurriedly wrapped the gun back up and put it in a book bag he found laying on the basement floor to keep his aunt and little cousin from seeing it.

"Are you OK Lil C?" Inquired Ms. Jones

"Yes Auntie, I'm fine. I think I'm just about ready to go." Before leaving Lil C gathered all the pictures he could find of his parents and put them in his bag as well.

Ms. Jones got all Lil C's clothes taken out to the car. "Are you sure that's all you want for now? We probably won't be coming back for a couple of days." Glancing the room one more time.

"Yes, ma'am. I got everything I need." In the back of his mind thinking to himself, all he needed was the pictures he gathered and the gun.

"So does this mean you're gonna live with us forever?" I asked Xavier in hopes for this to be the case.

Giving Xavier a nudge. "Yeah Lil cuz. That's what this means. I'm living with ya'll forever." Walking to the car.

CHAPTER 3

That night shortly after they arrived back at the house Lil C and Xavier went to their room. Usually, they would just cut off the lights and go to sleep on their separate bunks, but this night was different. C sat on Xavier's bed next to him. "I know you're young and don't know a lot about what's going on, but I'm gonna tell you. Just keep it between us OK?" Reaching his hand out to receive a shake in agreement. "I know I told everybody I didn't know who killed my parents but that's not the truth. I lied because I didn't think ya'll would be safe if I told you."

"Do you think they still wanna kill you?"

"I think they would kill all of us to keep from going to jail, but I'm not gonna let that happen."

"What you gonna do?"

Shaking his head. "I can't say. But what I can say is by the time you wake up in the morning they won't be able to hurt us ever again. I promise." Lil C tucked Xavier in and picked up the alarm clock which read ten forty and set the alarm for two o'clock before laying down himself. "In a couple of hours, I'm gonna make all this go away." He said under his breath as he put the cover over his head. Time felt like it was barely moving to Lil C, who peeked at the clock every few minutes waiting for the hour to come for him to put his plan in motion. Seeing the time saying one-thirty. "That's close enough." Lil C cancels the alarm and get's out of bed putting on all black clothes, repeatedly whispering to himself. "It's on until it's over. It's on until it's over." Trying to give himself an extra boost. Before walking out he leaned down over Xavier and said. "If anything happens to me tonight you gotta be the man and take care of your mom." Not really expecting a response. "I love you little cuz." Getting out of the house unnoticed was easy being Ms. Jones was a heavy sleeper thanks to her nightly muscle relaxers. Once outside Lil C threw his bookbag over his shoulder, hopped on his bike, and pedaled away. The whole ride to Red's house he imagined how everything was going to play out in his mind. Telling his self this was going to be a piece of cake when really he was just as scared of Red as he was that night.

When Lil C arrived at Red's house he noticed that all the lights were off except for the bedroom light. He removed the gun from his bag and cocked it. Crawling alongside the house making sure to stay below the windows C came to Red's bedroom window. He could see Red sitting straight up on the bed with his back against the headboard and his head drooping down as if he fell asleep watching television. "It's now or never." Lil C says under his breath as he stands up and takes aim at Red. Freezing up briefly as he pictured this man pistol-whipping his dad and raping his mom.

Red lifts his head and opens his eyes in time to see the muzzle flash from Lil C's gun. "What the fuck!" Seeing the first shot barely missed his head, Red reaches to his nightstand to grab his gun he had laying there only it was too late. The next two shots hit Red ripping through his chest and stomach.

Lil C stood in shock and watched Red squirm around on the bed until he took his last breath. "That's for my parents!" Running back to his bike Lil C pedaled as fast as he could to Saint's house, which was just a couple blocks from where Red lived.

Lil C knows Saint's house like the back of his hand because his dad had been bringing him here with him since he was a baby. Saint had three big rottweilers that guarded his house. Two that he let Rome the backyard at all times named Face and Mask. And Bruno who was the largest of the three stayed inside. Now although these dogs were trained to be savage killers, that didn't scare Lil C one bit for the reason he has been around all three dogs since they were pups. He just patted their huge heads after jumping the fence and they practically escorted him to the back door, where he retrieved a key Saint kept hidden under a flowerpot. As soon as he entered the house Bruno met him at the door. "Good boy, Good boy." He patted Bruno's head and let him outside to join Face and Mask. Wasting no time Lil C went straight to Saint's room turning on the light as he enters with his gun pointed at Saint and his wife Laura, who is in bed.

"What the fuck?" Saint shouted as he adjust his eyes to the light. "Do you know what you're doing with that nephew? Seeing the coldness in Lil C's expression. "Put that down and let's talk. I'm sure we can figure this out together."

"Yeah C put the gun down." Exclaimed Laura in fear.

Lil C didn't say a word he just stared into Saint's face as he pointed his gun.

His unresponsiveness has Saint on edge. "Look nephew I can give you anything you want." Pointing at a stack of money he had lying on his dresser. "Besides if you kill me do you know how many people will be looking for you. That aunt of yours can't protect you. I'ma send Red over there to treat her like he did your whore momma!"

Without a word Lil C squeezed the trigger repeatedly until his gun cocked back, shooting Saint in his face and chest multiple times. Laura screamed hysterically as she watched her husband's murderer escape into the dark of the night.

Pedaling as fast as he could to the cemetery, Lil C hopped off his bike when he got to his parent's grave and collapsed to his knees. "I did it! It's over!" Yelled Lil C. "They're gone for good!" Sitting with his back against his parent's headstone, Lil C just rocked and talked to himself throughout the rest of the night.

CHAPTER 4

Bang, Bang, Bang! Bang, Bang, Bang! Ms. Jones was awakened by a series of loud knocks on her door. "I'm coming!" She yelled as she wrapped her robe around her body. Bang, Bang, Bang! "I said I'm coming." Yelling even louder "What in God's name is going on." Under her breath. As soon as she enters the hallway she can see Xavier peeking out to see what's going on. "Get your butt back in there and close your door!"

Bang, Bang, Bang! "This is Warren PD open the door or we will be forced to kick it in!" An officer's voice came through the door.

Ms. Jones opened her door to see ten officers with their guns drawn. Putting her hands in the air. "What is going on officer?"

Trying to look past Ms. Jones as he barged in, the leading officer says. "We've got a warrant for Carl Jones. Where is he?"

"My nephew hasn't done anything. He's in his bed where he's been all night. C, get out here!"Looking towards the bedroom.

Xavier who is still peeking out yells back. "He's not in here mom!"

With a shocked look on her face. "What do you mean he's not in there?"

"He left mommy. When I was asleep he left."

"Where did he go?" Ms. Jones snatched Xavier by the arms and looked him in his eyes and as calm of a voice as she could muster. "Xavier if you know anything, you need to tell me right now."

Not really understanding what's going on. "He just said he was going to make sure the men that killed Uncle Carl and Aunt Harriet don't come back and kill us."

Embracing Xavier. "Please Lord protect my nephew." Ms. Jones turns her attention to the officer. "Please tell me what is going on." Breathing deeply, trying to calm herself.

"Well, Ms. Jones… We received a call that a young man that the caller named to be Carl Jones, had shot her husband last night."

Looking doubtful. "And who is this lady's husband?"

"Robert Santose." Stated the officer.

"Saint?" Questioned Ms. Jones in disbelief.

"Yes, ma'am. I have been told that he also goes by that name." Confirmed the officer.

Standing with her mouth gaped in total awe, Ms. Jones tries to process this information. "I'm sorry officer but as you see my nephew is not here. I got to get out there and find him." Rushing the officers out.

"I totally understand and I apologize we had to put you through this so early, but can you promise me that if you hear from Carl that you'll give me a call. It will be in his best interest." Handing her a card. "My name is Officer Daniels."

"Don't worry I will call you immediately. Thank you for letting me know what's going on." Watching the police pull off before frantically running to her room. "Xavier throw on the clothes you had on last night! Hurry up! We gotta go!" Yelling to Xavier who is still in his room.

Ms. Jones came out of her room to see Xavier dressed and waiting at the door. "I was ready fast momma. Is C OK?"

"I pray to God he is but we have to find him." Ms. Jones pulled out the driveway so fast she could see Xavier slide across the seat. "Sorry baby... put your seatbelt on." Placing her hand on her forehead." I'm just moving at a hundred miles per hour." Taking a deep breath. "Lord God you know I ain't ready to lose another one." After driving around Warren for an hour Ms. Jones is running out of places to look. "Xavier I need you to think real hard for me."

Looking up at his mom. "Yes, ma'am. About what?"

"You talk to Lil C all the time. Is there anywhere he would go if he were mad or sad or scared?"

"He's not scared of nothin ever. But when he be mad he always say he wanna go sit with his parents and talk. I always tell him he's crazy, cause they're in the cemetery." Not realizing he was really saying something.

"Oh my God! Oh my God! That's it! I love you so much." Looking back at Xavier. Picking up speed. Ms. Jones headed to the cemetery. When she pulled she could see C slumped over next to the headstone. Jumping out the car. "C! C!" She screamed as she ran to him as fast as she could, grabbing him and squeezing him so tightly. "Are you okay?"

"Yes ma'am, I'm okay." Squeezing her back. "I got them, Auntie. They can't hurt us no more." Sobbing.

Ms. Jones stepped back and examined Lil C up and down. "Where's the gun?" Holding her hand out.

C held open his bag showing her the gun inside. "It don't got no more bullets. I ran out."

Ms. Jones is paralyzed with shock as she realized the gun that is in the bag. Quickly zipping it closed, Ms. Jones placed it in her trunk. As she pulled out of the cemetery she saw two police cars. "Get down C!" Driving calmly past. "They got police everywhere looking for you… what happened?"

Lil C taking a deep breath before answering. "Do you remember how I said I didn't know who shot me and my parents? Watching her nod in agreement. "Well, I lied. I saw everything. I saw Red smacking my dad around with his gun then he shot him in the head. Then he beat my mom up. Then raped her. The whole time she was screaming and trying to fight. Then he shot her in the head."

"What about Butch. How did he get shot?"

"He was on top of me the whole time covering my mouth while Red did what he did." By now his tears are flowing as he talks. "Red told Butch to kill me, but instead he kept telling Red I was too young for the octopus arm. Then Red shot him and he fell on top of me. Like I couldn't move or nothing. I remember he told me he was sorry and to stay down. Then I felt something hit me on my side really hard. I guess that's when he shot me." Asking curiously. "Do you know what he meant when he kept sayin I was too young for the octopus arm? Because whatever it meant he tried to save my life for it."

"Well, honey, as crazy as he was, Butch was always a person with rules, and I thank God for that. But he got that saying because when we were younger at the amusement park, to get on the most dangerous roller coaster... You had to be taller than the octopus arm. And none of us were tall enough. And your Uncle Butch was so mad he yelled at the guy that worked the ride.. he said... We're gonna ride this ride anyway." Trying to mock Butch's high pitched man voice. "What you gonna do?" And he looked Butch dead in the eye and he said... I ain't gonna do nothing. This ride is gonna throw ya'll in all sorts of directions to ya'lls death because ya'll ain't big enough for the octopus arm... And I swear if that didn't stick with him."

"Why do you think they did that? My dad would do anything for anybody. My mom too."

"Well, you have to understand that some people are just bad. Their spirits, their conversations, their presence. And even though they spoiled you with everything those guys are known to be monsters in the streets. Real killers. As you get older you'll be able to distinguish the good from the bad because smiles can make it confusing." Looking back at Lil C. "I don't want to see anything happen to you, but I can't let you run forever."

Lil C looked over at Xavier who had fallen asleep and dropped his head. "Yes, ma'am... I know. My dad always said only cowards hide. And I ain't no coward. He said that when a man gotta stand up for whatever he believes is right and sometimes that meant getting dealt with. I don't think I was wrong for killing them so I ain't scared of what's gonna happen. I'm just happy to know they can't hurt any of us ever again."

Ms. Jones looked at C thoughtfully. "You keep saying them. The police told me Saint got killed. But you keep saying them. Did you? Oh my." Ms. Jones stopped realizing Lil C had killed more than Saint.

"Yes, Auntie. I killed Red and Saint."

"Did anyone see you kill Red?"

"No, ma'am. He was by himself. They probably haven't found him yet."

"C you know they're gonna lock you up for a long time for this."

"I know but I really don't care. No matter how long I get, my parents ain't gonna come back."

They both became quiet and stayed that way for, while Ms. Jones drove. Lil C is finally at peace.

CHAPTER 5

A couple of days after Lil C turned himself in, he is paid a visit by an attorney. "How are you doing Carl?" Offering Lil C a handshake before sitting at the table across from him. "It's really good to finally meet you. Now with your permission, I would like to represent you throughout your trial."

"Did my aunt send you to me?"

"No, actually I was sent to you by Mr. Lupino. He told me to do whatever I could to either get you off or get you the lightest sentence possible." Crossing his fingers on the table.

Uncertain. "Let me talk to my aunt cause she gotta pay for everything and I don't really know how all this works."

"Well let me start by breaking down to you exactly how this works." He clears his throat and pushes his glasses up on his nose. "You can not let me represent you and you can get some second rate lawyer in the area who doesn't give a rats ass about you, or even worst-case scenario, a public defender. In either case, they're both going to just tell you to take the first thing the courts throw at you which will end up with you probably spending the rest of your childhood and most of your adult life in prison. Or you can let me do what I'm known to do, as I am the best around here and see if we can't get you back out in the world as soon as possible. I'm not going to beat around the bush with you kid. You're facing some real serious charges." Looking back down at his notes. "Two counts aggravated murder. One count breaking and entering. One count of tampering with evidence."

"How did I tamper with evidence?" Looking befuddled.

"Well, there is no report of them receiving the murder weapon which leads them to believe that you hid it to avoid being caught." Trying to be clear.

"That's stupid." Scoffs Lil C.

"I agree, it is stupid but that's how it goes. They're also going to probably try to prove that the whole thing was premeditated because of what happened before these two."

"What does that mean?"

"In a nutshell, it means I'm the best option you got. Besides Mr. Lupino already paid me in full for everything and your aunt knows all about me. I was your father's lawyer for years. Since way before you were born."

Shrugging his shoulders. "I guess I can't say no then. But why did Mr. Lupino pay for everything?"

"Now that right there is a million-dollar question that only he can answer." Standing up from the table and extending his hand out to Lil C once again. "It's a pleasure to be able to help you. I'll be seeing you real soon."

After thirteen drawn-out months of going back and forth with the prosecution, Mr. Speary gets them to agree to give Lil C juvenile life instead of being charged as an adult.

CHAPTER 6

The sun has never shined so bright or felt so warm as it did this day. The wind has never sounded so clear as it rustled through the leaves. Lil C can't help but appreciate mother nature's beauty as he sat at the bus stop waiting on his Aunt Carol to pick him up. It's been little over a year since he's seen his Aunt and about three years since he's seen his cousin Xavier.

"I wonder if he got any bigger. "Lil C pondered to himself as he pictured the last time his little cousin visited him. Watching every car that pulled into the station, Lil C was getting more and more anxious to see his aunt pull up. "Damn it's hot as a bitch out here!" He says as he walks into the station to get a drink of water from the fountain.

"You waiting on somebody young fella?" Came a strange yet familiar voice from behind him as he bent over to sip.

"Xavier!" Lil C shouts his name as he turns to embrace him. Standing back to view Xavier's whole body. "Damn you done got big as hell boy!"

"Look who's talkin," Xavier says looking up at Lil C who is now standing six foot four, weighing two hundred fifty pounds solid muscle. "You're not getting called Lil C ever again." They both laugh.

"Where's your mom?" C asked as he looks around.

"She's outside waiting in the truck." Pointing out the window. "She said she didn't wanna get out in the heat. Plus we weren't sure you made it here yet or not."

"Shit I don't care if the bus would've broken down, I would've got out and walked. But I definitely was gonna be here when ya'll got here." Throwing his arm over Xavier's shoulders. "So you said Auntie got a truck?"

"Yeah, she got a Cherokee. It's alright. I like Tahoes."

"Look at ya'll coming up. I miss you little cuz!" Giving Xavier a shake. "Man let's get out here before Auntie starts trippin."

Ms. Carol jumped out of the truck as soon as she saw them come out of the station. In tears. "My baby!" She ran towards C with her arms out. "My baby's home!"

As they hug, C whispers in Ms. Carol's ear. 'It's over Auntie… It's all over."

"Thank you, Lord Jesus!" She shouted as she hugged C.

"Mom, you're gonna be able to hug him forever. We gotta go get the rest of the stuff." Rushing them.

Talking over Ms. Carol's shoulder. "Boy, stop hatin. She can hug me as long as she wants." Mocking Xavier. "We gotta go get the rest of the stuff."

"I just can't believe how tall you've gotten." Ms. Carol said looking up at C.

"Thanks to Mr. Lupino I was eatin good in there." Rubbing his washboard stomach.

Coming to her mind. "Speaking of Mr. Lupino, he wants me to bring you by the store on our way home. That man thinks so much of you. He's definitely been a blessing to have in our corner through all this." Glancing the parking lot. "Well, I guess we won't be seeing anyone, just standing around here. Xavier open that hatch so C can throw his bag in there."

"Yes, ma'am." Xavier can see his mom fiddling with the radio from the back of the truck. "Ma, put it on the CD so I can let C hear some of my beats." As they approach the car doors. "You can sit up here. I just gotta grab my stuff."

Brushing him off with a hand gesture. "You sit up there. I just wanna look out my window and chill…. Besides you gotta be the DJ" C started bobbing his head immediately when the music starts playing. "Whoooo! Stop shy truthin. That ain't you!"

"What? You are crazy if that ain't me. This all I do!" Turning down the radio. "Ma… Can you tell your nephew I'm nice? I'm gonna be the next Dr. Dre." Turning the volume up to max.

"You're going to be the next beat up kid on the side of the road if you don't turn my speakers down some!" Looking in her rearview mirror back at C. "But that's really him. I keep telling him he needs to be making beats for the church"

Xavier, blurting over her. "Could you imagine the choir coming out dancing to this?" Doing a hip-hop dance while singing the words to Jesus is real to his beat. "Sometimes when I'm feeling low, nowhere to go, Jesus comes along and, Ouch!"

C reached over the seat and popped Xavier in the back of the head. "You jeefin for real little dude. But on the real, I got flows for days so you gonna have to let me spit something over one of your beats."

"We can make some music today!" Assured Xavier. "I got everything we need to record in my room." Giving C a wink. "Clear audio too."

Dancing in his seat. "Don't tell me that cause it's about to go down round these parts for real!"

After a few more minutes of music talk, they pulled up to Lupino's. C lead the way into the store. "I heard you were lookin for me old man," C says noticing Mr. Lupino's backside as he arranges the cigarettes.

"Lil C!" Mr. Lupino hurries around the counter and puts his hands on C's shoulders. "I can't believe my eyes! You went in that place a little boy and now look at you. I don't know if I can call you Little C anymore."

C flexing his chest as he speaks. "Yeah… we came to that conclusion on the way over here. I'm dropping the little. Smiling from ear to ear.

"Well, that is a decision well earned." Patting C on the shoulder. "How long you been home for?"

"I just got off the bus and my aunt brought me straight here."

Mr. Lupino looking as if he just realized Ms. Carol and Xavier were standing there. "Now, Now, Look at my manors. My apologies Carol. I was just so excited to see C I lost my brain."

"You don't have to apologize. I was blown away when I first saw him too. " Comforts Ms. Carol.

"Do you have any plans for the next hour or so?" Asked Mr. Lupino.

Answering slowly, looking at his aunt. "No…I don't think I do."

"Well, what do you say you hang out with me for a spell and I'll run you home after. I just want to talk to you for a little bit." They both look at Ms. Carol.

Throwing her hands up. "I don't mind at all. Besides I got a few more stops to make before I go home. Just call me when your on your way to make sure I'm there." Ms. Carol hugged C again and she and Xavier walked out of the store.

"So how's it feel to be a free man?" Mr. Lupino asked as he turned his open sign around to close on his door.

"I mean, I'm glad to be out and all. But I got some things to figure out on some grown man shit…. Oh, my bad." Realizing he swore.

"C… After what you been through you deserve to be able to say anything you want."

"With that being said I wanna say thank you so much for looking out for me through everything. If there's anything I can do for you just let me know. I owe you whatever you want after this."

"Follow me." Mr. Lupino leads the way to the back of the store, and down the basement steps. When they reached the bottom he flipped the light switch revealing a room that resembled a mini disco club. It had a few tables, a fully stocked bar, and even a little area for dancing, with red lights hanging overhead. "Man, me and your dad used to come down here all the time and throw private parties. I really miss your dad. He was a great man. He was such a good man that you don't owe me nothing. I hope that made me right with him." Grabbing two beers out of the mini-fridge.

"Wow!" C looks around the room astonished. "This room always been down here?

"Yeah, this room was always here before you were born. Let me ask you a serious question… I know you were young when your parents got killed but do you know what your father did for a living?"

Cringing his face from his first taste of beer. "I mean, I know that he and Saint was supposed to have their own business. And one time when we were having a job day he told me he didn't wanna come and talk about boring sales stuff. So I always assumed whatever they were selling had to be worth a lot for everything to have happened the way it did."

"Worth a lot? That's saying it lightly." Sitting a bag of coke on the bar in front of C. "Do you know what this is?"

"Man! Is this real? I've seen this on t.v. but never in real life." Adding up the facts. "Hold up. Are you saying my dad was a drug dealer?"

Speaking nonchalantly. "Well, I guess that could be one title you could call it. But I looked at him as nothing less than a businessman. It came down to greed is why they killed your dad. I think Saint felt that by killing your dad, he could keep everything instead of the fifty fifty split they had been doing." Sipping his beer. "As soon as I found out Saint had your parents killed I cut all ties with him and told him he was unloyal. That didn't sit well with him so he was heard making some threats on me which lead me to put one hundred thousand dollars on Saint's head and fifty thousand dollars on Red's." Leaning in to whisper to C as if there were someone else in the room. "Who would've ever imagined that a thirteen-year-old boy would get to them before five of the states' most deadly killers. So back to what you said about owing me, I think I owe you. You did me such a service."

"No disrespect Mr. Lupino. But I didn't kill them for you at all. I killed them because they took my parents from me and I knew that they weren't gonna let me live knowing there was a chance of me remembering something. Seeing how Red did me and my parents I knew that they would kill anyone around me and I couldn't let them hurt anyone else I love. And more than all that I was hoping it would make my dreams of that night go away."

"Did they go away?"

"Only when I'm awake."

"C you've been through so much. What do you want to do now that all that's behind you?"

Looking around as if the answer were written on the walls. "I don't know. I just know I gotta get some money to get a car and my own place and I'ma figure the rest out from there."

"Let me set you up." Placing a gym bag on the bar. Unzipping it to expose some money. "Like I said I owe you. This is your hundred thousand. I'm going to give you five bricks to get you started and the other fifty I owe you. Those things you want are already yours. I want you to have everything you want for the rest of your life."

"And what's to assure me that I won't run into the same type of fate my father had?"

Shrugging his shoulders. "There's no guarantee you won't. But not to say anything bad about your father, I always told him he was too nice to people. And in this game, people often mistake kindness for weakness. He also insisted on making Saint his partner, and he put too much trust in him. I always told him that there ain't no such thing as partners or equals in this. If you shine too bright the next man is going to either want what you got or want to be who you are. Back to rule numero uno… Trust no one but yourself! Don't keep any product around you. And if you can help it, don't have your place of residence anywhere near your place of business. Dealing where you live is like shitting where you sleep. I gave your father this exact talk when he was a little bit younger than you and he chose his cards. Now I can't take nothing away from him neither. He played a hell of a hand, but I just can't help but think if he would've listened to me. I'd still have my best friend. But that was your dad. No one could tell him anything. He was a man by his own command. He lived his life his way and that was just the way it was."

Unsettled. "I don't know nothing about this shit."

"Look C... If you want to go home and think about it for a few days I understand. But just know that I'm not going to just throw you to the wolves. I'm going to have my nephew get with you and set you up with some good people who are going to buy everything from you. All you have to do is wait on the call and make the drop. I'm going to get you a place to live and a place to hustle from. You pay the rent at the place you live after the first three months and I'll split the rent with you in the spot you hustle from for as long as you stay on board. You pay all the utilities in both units." Putting the bag of money in a safe under the bar. "Regardless of what you choose this is your money. I'm going to keep it here for you until we get you set up. I don't think it would be in either of our best interests for you to repeat anything we spoke about tonight. And don't let nobody know how much money you got. These little motherfuckers are wolves out here and before you can defend yourself against them eating you alive you're going to have to sit back and watch how they move from every angle." Tapping C on the shoulder. "You get what I'm trying to say to you kid?"

"I totally get what you're trying to say. And I thank you. I don't gotta think about it. My father trusted you and I just feel I should trust you too."

Mr. Lupino bent down and grabbed two more beers out of the minifridge. "I know you were young when you went in there, but is this your first time drinking beer?"

After chugging the rest of his first bottle down, C spun the second bottle in his hand reading the label. "Well I tasted my dad's Old English before, but that was just a sip. I never had my own bottle before."

Holding his bottle in the air. "I wanna make a toast to you coming home and finding your presence at the top well needed. And that you give these streets everything your father did and then some. You're like my own family and I love you C. It's your time." They toast and Mr. Lupino hands C his phone. "Call your aunt and let her know we're gonna be heading her way shortly."

CHAPTER 7

The moon had taken over the sun's existence by the time C and Mr. Lupino left the store. The city he had been telling his friends about for the past five years seems to have been replaced by something similar but just not quite as he remembered it. The ride from the store to his aunt's house was the same path he remembered, but the houses looked different to him. "It's crazy cause I knew the whole way where to turn and everything, but everything just looks different."

"Well C. Things have been getting run down. There weren't this many boarded-up houses when you left and some of the houses you probably remember have been torn down."

Pulling into the driveway, Mr. Lupino notices all the lights are off in the house. "It doesn't look like anyone's home yet. If you want we can sit here and wait."

She told me the back door would be unlocked when I called her." Taking off his seatbelt. "Thanks for everything, Mr. Lupino. I really don't know how everything would be for me right now if it weren't for you." Extending his hand.

"As long as we take care of each other Young C, everything's going to be o.k. Now hows about you let this old man use your bathroom. These beers are trying their best to get out."

"Sure, Mr. Lupino. We just gotta go the back way through the gate." As they entered the house C thought he heard something move in the living room. "I don't know what that was but stay right here."

"Surprise!" The light came on in the living room and C notices two of his friends that he used to play with before everything happened. There were also about six people standing there that C didn't recognize.

"Welcome home nigga!" Sam said as he grabbed C's hand and embraced him with a one-arm hug.

"Yeah boy! You already know it's about to go down!" Paul said as he welcomed his friend as well. "It seems like forever since we seen your ass! Man, you got big as hell boy!" Covering his mouth. "Oops sorry about that Ms. Jones."

"I'll let it slide this time Paul due to the circumstances, but you know I don't have all that cussing in my house." Rubbing her index finger over the other to shame him. "C, let me introduce you to a couple of people you don't know." Pointing around the room. "This is Susan, Anne, Lisa, Tish, and Andrea. I work with all these crazy ladies and I talk about you so much that they wanted to help me throw you something special when you came home." Pointing at the last person in the room. "And this here is Bernadette. She was Xavier's babysitter for a while."

C gestures to everyone. Well, it is really nice meeting all of you and thanks for coming over." Looking at Bernadette. "And I really wanna thank you for coming out. You are just what I needed to see today."

Bernadette gave C a bashful smile. "And why is that?"

"Let's just say I have a lot of plans but no one to share them with."

"And how does meeting me change any of that?" Putting her hand on her hip.

Rethinking his wording. "How about what do I have to do to chill with you one day to show you what I mean? I ain't trying to disrespect you but I swear you are beautiful."

"Well thank you, but I'm gonna be honest with you. We can be friends and all but I have a boyfriend, so us dating or anything is not about to happen."

"Do you love your dude?"

Sassily. "What kind of question is that? It's my boyfriend ain't it?"

Speaking sure of himself. "It was really supposed to be an easy question if you did love him. But check this out. I know I just got out and you probably think I'm just talking shit, but I'ma get on my feet real soon. And after I get all the way right I'm coming to get you. That's my word. No shy truthin."

"Well as you said you just came home. And I do think your just talking stuff. So what do you say you just focus on getting you right." Patting C on the chest as she walked off into the kitchen.

C just smiled as he watched her walk away. "Yeah I need that in my life." Under his breath.

Sam bumped into C. "Snap out of it homeboy. There's plenty more to see. Trust me. Besides she is all about her nigga."

"Man fuck that. I'ma make her all about me. She fine as hell." C looked back into the kitchen to catch another glance at her.

"Hey, why don't you step outside with me and Paul real quick so we can smoke." After they get outside Sam pulls out a big blunt and lights it. "Here C hit this."

Brushing him off. "I don't even know how to inhale that shit. I tried once in jail."

Paul snatched the blunt out of Sam's hand. "It's easy just do this." Taking a big pull, Paul let a cloud of smoke come halfway out of his mouth before swallowing it all back in. trying not to let any smoke out as he spoke. "Hold it in for a few seconds then breathe it out slow." Handing C the blunt. "Now you try."

"Man ya'll gonna have me fucked up out here." C hit the blunt as Paul had shown him but instead of holding in the smoke he began coughing violently.

Taking the blunt out of C's hand. "Welcome to the world of hydro," Sam says before taking a pull. "Hey, on the real, I can put you on with some of this if you wanna get your pockets right. Muthafuckas buy this shit like it was crack." Passing the blunt to Paul. "Now ounces go for two fifty but I can get them for two all day and that's what you'll pay."

"Sounds good and all but I'ma pass for right now. But on another note." Tilting his head sideways. "Ya'll muthafuckas look funny as fuck right now." C started laughing so hard his eyes began to tear up.

Pointing at C. "This nigga high as hell." Says Paul.

Xavier comes out of the back door. "What ya'll doing?"

C put his hands up in his fight stance. "We just talkin bout how we were gonna jump you if you came outside. What you doin?"

"I was getting bored sitting there with all my mom's friends."

"Hey C we gotta bust. I got money to make." Sam said as he dapped C up before walking to his car.

Paul dapped C up as well. "Whenever you wanna step out and kick it give us a call. You can get our numbers from your aunt."

Waving his friends off. "Ya'll be safe out there." After watching them pull off C turns to Xavier. "So little cuz what's really been up with you?"

Shrugging his shoulders. "Nothing really. I've just mostly been in my room making music."

"You don't got no girlfriend?"

"No. Most of the girls at my school only talk to boys who got a lot of money."

"So what you saying... You need a lot of money to talk to a girl? Boy, do we got some work to do."

"I ain't worried about it cause when this music blow, I'ma have all the girls jocking me."

"So what's the deal with that chick Bernadette's boyfriend?"

Peeking in the door to make sure no one was listening. "Tony? For real. That dude is crazy. My mom doesn't know I know but I heard my mom on the phone with her, talking about how he hits her. And I mean all the time."

Showing his rage. "What! And she don't wanna holler at me? It's all good. I got a plan that's gonna set us all straight. And I'm talking about enough money to buy any gold-digging bitch you want. And I swear I'ma get Bernadette on my team. Just give me a little time to put some things in motion."

CHAPTER 8

Seven years later and several keys greater, C has acquired everything Mr. Lupino promised and more. He supplies all the major drug dealers in Warren, Youngstown, Akron and parts of Cleveland. He also buys pounds of weed which he fronts to Xavier who now goes by X. Life has become everything he wanted it to be.

Looking around his room as if he had never seen it before. Big C awakens from a reoccurring dream he's been haunted with since the murder of his parents. Without any hesitation he grabs the blunt he fell asleep on, out of his ashtray next to his bed. "Now I see why I couldn't fuck with you." He said looking at the blunt astonished by how fat he rolled it. Sparking it up. "Wake and bake X! Wake and bake!" He yells

X's agitated voice comes from the living room. "You better get the fuck on wit that bullshit! It's too early for all that!"

Laughing at the mood he's put his little cousin in. "You better watch how you talk to me little dude and come hit this L!" Changing his voice to a more patient tone. "Besides I need to holla at you real quick."

"What you need to holla at me about?" X asked curiously as he made his way from the living room.

Seeing X enter the room C reaches the blunt out to him. "I need to talk about my balls in your jaws sucka." Dropping his feet to the floor to make room for X to sit. "What would you say if I told you I'm making one more trip and when that runs out I'm done?"

"Man… I'd have to say it sounds like you had another one of your dreams again. You always say your quitting and as soon as you make a couple thousand, you change your mind. I think we should have this talk after you've thought about it some more."

Pushing X's arm. "I'm serious Lil cuz. This shit got me stressed out. I can't chill with my family. And more than anything I just wanna do me without having to worry about making sure everybody's straight."

Placing his hand over his heart. "Damn bro. You got me feeling some type of way. Don't let me keep you in the game. I'ma be o.k." In a mocking manner.

"Man, you trippin. I'm not just talking about you. I'm talkin bout everybody. Let's say right now today I just disappear. Where's everybody gonna get their dope from?" C gave X the eye as if he was giving him a chance to respond. "Exactly! So I feel I have to keep this Muthafuckin roller coaster ride open for all customers that's tall enough." Stopping in mid-sentence and pointing at X.

"For the octopus arm. I get it. Cause you've been like a hood superhero. And who's gonna save all the crackheads if you weren't around?" Ridiculed X.

"You got jokes but you think these fiends be trippin now. Just imagine them without being able to get they fix. It'll be like a junky Apocolypse out this bitch." They both break out laughing. "But seriously… I got enough money put up. I got people lined up to take on certain responsibilities. I pretty much got this whole thing mapped out to run without me. That's what I been waiting on. Trying to figure out how to get out but keep everybody straight."

"So what are you going to do when you're out?" Questioned X.

Looking baffled. "Nigga…. Did you hear a single word I said? Chill with my family! Do me! I can't walk you through every step of my future. I just know it won't consist of this shit."

"I feel you." Looking at the monitor to see someone pull up on a bike. "Lester's crack head ass is about to be at the door. Want me to let him in?"

"Hell yeah, he right on time. Take him in the kitchen and tell him to get started cleaning up and I'll be out in a second."

Opening the door. "Lester the dope tester. C said go ahead and get started cleaning the kitchen and he'll be right out."

Mumbly speaking. "I got some nice jewelry for you to give your girl." Pulling a few tangled necklaces out of his pocket. "Just let me get them apart."

"Nah, I'm good. You need to give that raggedy shit back to whoever you stole it from cause that's the only person that thinks it's worth something."

"You in here harassing my cousin again Lester," C says as he enters the kitchen. "And what I tell you bout coming over here selling shit. I'm the only motherfucka to sell anything in this bitch. I don't give a fuck what it is. You gonna make me rob your old ass."

Frustrated. "Man, ain't nobody doing nothing to this little pipsqueak. I'm just trying to look out for ya'll like ya'll look out for me."

C laughing. "You always a slick talkin motherfucka, ain't you."

"I'm just trying to keep ya'll boys on point." Responds Lester.

"Well, when you're done within here I'ma have you cut the grass. I'm about to run some errands. This is half of what I'ma owe you." C hands Lester two pieces of crack. "If I ain't back by the time you finish hit my phone and I'ma pull up on you." Turning to X. "You wanna ride with me to the store?"

"Damn right. I need to go to the store anyways. My mouth is dry as a bitch."

C pointing at Lester. "Make sure you lock my shit up cause if anything comes up missing, you know it's gonna be your head I'm after."

"Man you know I wouldn't steal from you."

"Maybe not today, but I don't trust your ass. What I do trust is my ability to make you suffer if you do. I'll catch you in a little bit." C and X walk out of the house.

CHAPTER 9

The early bird gets the worm is the motto. So even though it's barely nine o'clock the store parking lot is busy like it's lunch hour. The young block hustlers are running up to every car that slows down, hoping it will be their next big sell. While the older crew shoots craps against the store wall. You had to have time served on the block, as well as money and respect to even touch the dice with these guys. But as with anything, there's always an exception. And in this case, the exception was Joe Joe. He is only thirteen and looks even younger. He has been on the block hustling since he was ten. He's been in and out of juvenile and has already made a reputation for himself to be a shooter.

Joe Joe seeing his point land on the dice. "You might as well just hand over all your money and save yourself the embarrassment of me taking it all from you on these dice." Picking up his winnings.

"Fuck you! With your little young ass. Shoot a hundred." Stacey says challenging Joe Joe.

Joe Joe smirks while dropping two fifties. "I'll be young while I'm bucking your ass." Rolling the dice. "Buck! Buck!" I told you I was hot now I got a fever."

"Be-bet fi-fifty you don't five nine." Stuttered Tank. He might have a problem with his words but this short cocky pitbull looking dude doesn't have a problem knocking people out. Or talking shit while doing it.

"I can't fade it." Joe Joe said as he pushed Tank's money back towards him.

"I got you faded on that fifty." Said Peewee. Peewee is six foot six and looks like a linebacker in the NFL, but he talks with the voice of a mouse. He and Tank are best friends and known as the crashers because every time they get drunk at a party, they turn it into a brawl. "Look here, motherfucker… You're gonna stop standing so close behind me like you trying to go in my pockets or something." Peewee snapped looking over his shoulder at Tyrone, who wasn't placing any bets.

"Man, ain't nobody on what you on," Tyrone says as he walks away.

"Come on two three like Jordan!" Shouted Joe Joe as he rolled a seven. "Fuck! I guess it wouldn't be right for me to take all your money anyways. I have only been rolling for twenty minutes straight. Who gonna put down with Stacy so I can run in the store quickly."

"I got your fi-fi-fifty." Stuttered Tank.

"That's a bet," Stacy confirms as he rolls his point.

As Joe Joe walks into the store he yells back out the door. "Ya'll better get all the money ya'll can cause when I get back on, I ain't getting off!"

"Don't be bringing all that shit in my store today!" Mace, the Arab behind the counter snapped at Joe Joe.

"Fuck you, Osama Bin shot ya. Give me a Snickers and a Payday." Joe Joe paid for his candy and headed out the store bumping into C as he walked in. "What's up C? Where's X at?"

"That nigga out in the car," C answered without looking back.

Joe Joe spotted C's car as soon as he got outside and walked straight to it and hops in the driver seat. Reaching his hand out. "What's good with your family? I thought you were going to come back thru last night. Aurie was getting on my nerves, asking where you were every ten minutes. Ya'll might as well stop playing and just be boyfriend and girlfriend. Everybody says that's your girl anyway."

"Back up boy. We good just like we are. But I went over C's and we got to smoking and next thing I know I was passed out on the couch." Looking around at everybody's motions. "I'm about to go home and get dressed. Then I got a couple of moves to make before trying to get up with you and smoke some of this hydro I got."

"I'm with that. Shit, I'm going to need something to help me make it through this day."

"What's wrong with your day?" X asked as if he knew it couldn't be serious.

"Shit what ain't wrong. The block jumping and I can't get no dope till later. Sid don't got no tree. And you're holding out on the drosky till you got time to fuck with your boy. The only thing that went good all morning is I got to buck them hoe ass niggas for a couple of dollars and that wasn't nothing but some chump change."

X just stared at Joe Joe for a couple of seconds before speaking. "You got your pistol on you?"

"Nah, but it won't be nothing for me to hop the fence and grab it. What's up? You trying to put in some work?" Joe Joe asked, ready for some action. "You know if my best friend got problems then I'm going to make his problems have problems."

Laughing at Joe Joe's seriousness. "It ain't nothing like that. I was just checking do I need to put you on suicide watch till I get back."

Joe Joe begins to laugh. "Fuck you, asshole. I ain't about to let the hood win that easy. I'll be right here getting it in when you come back." Seeing C getting impatient by the car. "Just make sure you don't bullshit like last night." Giving X dap before getting out.

After sitting in the car C blurts out. "I heard you talking. With as much shit you got going on out here you probably should keep your gun on you. Better have it and not need it, than to need it and not have it."

Joe Joe snaps back. "Don't act like you would give a fuck. You act like you to good than to put a nigga on. Like you scared I'ma take over or something."

C waves his finger at Joe Joe. "See I can tell just by how you talking to me that you ain't big enough for the octopus' arm. That's why I don't sell you shit. And don't think I don't know who you get your dope from. I'll drought that nigga out just to prove a point to you. And starve everybody that's eating with you. If I was you, I'd keep doing what I been doing until I holla at you. Not the other way around."

"Nigga fuck you and your octopus arm bitch!" Joe Joe in rage by C's remarks. "You ain't God out here nigga! I'm going to eat regardless! If I got to rob everybody, every day! Don't think you're untouchable!"

Jumping out of the car to his feet. "What the fuck you say to me? Boy, I'll beat your fucking ass!" Without any hesitation, C raised his hand and hit Joe Joe with a slap across his face knocking him to the ground. "I ain't one of these hoe ass niggas you be talking shit to all day."

X has run around the car and is helping Joe Joe to his feet. "What the fuck C? He's way younger than you!"

"I don't give a fuck how old he is! He keeps talking like he's big enough for the octopus' arm. I'm going to give it to him!" C jumped back into his car, screeching his tires as he backed out of the space. Holding the bag with X's eye drops out of the window. "Man, come get this! I'm good on ya'lls bullshit."

X jogged over to C's car and grabbed the bag. "Do you think I can get a sack till later when I break mine down?"

C cocked his head sideways in disbelief. "So, I'm supposed to give you a bag to smoke with this motherfucker after he just disrespected me? Nigga you just as crazy as he is. I don't know what the fuck you be thinking with this motherfucker!" Reaching under his headrest to pull out an eighth of hydro. "Here!" Handing X the weed. "And you better talk to your boy. I ain't about to keep letting shit slide cause he with you." C turned his music up and sped off down the street.

CHAPTER 10

X and Joe Joe watched C's car turn the corner and disappear, but they could still hear his music for a couple of minutes. "Man, I swear his shit be beating," X stated, not really considering what just happened.

"Man fuck that nigga's system! Old bitch ass nigga! I got something for his ass!" Spazzed Joe Joe.

"Ya'll gonna be alright. Ya'll both was on some bullshit. Besides I can't have my closest cousin and best friend beefing. Ya'll got to figure something out." X trying to make some sort of resolution. Patting his pockets. "You got a loose dollar so I can get a blunt. I only got twenties and I don't want to break them."

Reaching in his pocket to retrieve the dollar, Joe Joe notices he has blood on his shirt. "Fuck! Now my shirts all fucked up!" Holding his shirt out to show X. "I just bought this shirt!"

Trying to play down the situation. "Chill out with all that crying. We're about to go to your house to smoke. Just soak it in some cold water so it doesn't stain. As a matter of fact, after we smoke, I need you to roll with me to carry this entertainment stand in the house for my mom."

"I guess I can help you even though I shouldn't. I swear your mom doesn't like me either."

"It isn't that she doesn't like you. It's just she always be hearing bad stuff about you." X said as if it were reassuring.

"So, like I said. She doesn't like me." Reiterated Joe Joe.

Brushing off Joe Joe's remark. "Whatever you wanna think. I like you and that's all that matters. After smoking the blunt at Joe Joe's house, they headed to X's house. "Man, you look high as hell. Like your eyes are bleeding."

"How the fuck you think you look? Your eyes are bleeding too." Replied Joe Joe.

"Damn, I almost forgot I got these drops." X pulled the bottle of Visine out of his pocket and applied two drops to each eye before handing the bottle to Joe Joe who did the same.

"I don't know why you even try and cover up the fact that you're high. Your mom's gonna know what's up someday."

"It's a little thing called respect. Something you might not even know anything about." X looked up and saw his mother in the doorway, shaking her head with disappointment."

Joe Joe seeing the disappointment also. "I told you she didn't like me. Now she mad, you got me with you."

That's not why she's mad." Disagrees X.

Before he could get out why she was mad, Mrs. Carol shouts out to him. "What happened to ten o'clock?"

"I know momma and I'm sorry. It's just been a crazy morning. But I'm ready to go pick it up if you're ready. I even brought Joe Joe to help me."

"I swear it's always something with you when I need something done." Scorns Mrs. Jones.

"Joe Joe and C got into a fight." Immediately passing the buck.

Mrs. Jones looked at Joe Joe with her stern eyes. "Is this true what I'm hearing Joe Joe?"

Joe Joe is trying to sound as innocent as possible. "Yes, ma'am it's partly true."

"What do you mean partly? Either ya'll fought or ya'll didn't?" Questioned Mrs. Jones.

Joe Joe clears his throat. "Well we were disagreeing, and he took it upon his self to hit me because he didn't like what I had to say. I never tried to hit him back. If you ask me, he was just trying to be a bully."

"Now I don't condone him putting his hands, on you Joe Joe. But I can't help but feel like there's more to this story that you're not telling me. Besides from what I hear about you out here in these streets, you're not letting anyone bully you. Not even a little bit. So, you don't have to give me the you're a victim version. Besides I didn't hear you crying bully when you were out here beating up on Timmy last week."

"I didn't put my hands on him." Says Joe Joe.

"And I don't recall Timmy putting his hands on you either. All I'm trying to say is you can't be one way towards people, but then turn around and be mad because someone is the same way towards you. And don't think I'm saying C is right because I'm going to have some words with him as soon as I see him. Putting his hands on somebody's kid." Mrs. Carol began to speak under her breath.

In the middle of Mrs. Jones talking, Joe Joe started remembering to himself the day he got into a fight with Timmy. "What else is there for you to do out here other than getting money?" Snapped Joe Joe to Timmy.

"It ain't shit to do, but that don't mean I got to stand out here and catch a case with your ass." Answered Timmy.

"Do you got a bitch to lay up with?" Questioned Joe Joe.

Timmy confused by the question. "What the fuck you mean do I got a bitch to lay up with? Do you got a bitch to lay up with?"

Joe Joe snarls out his response. "I don't need a bitch to lay up with cause I'm out here getting money. Do you get it? Get money or get pussy. Or be pussy... Pussy!"

Timmy exploding with anger. "Bitch you're a pussy. You can suck my..."

Pow! Joe Joe lunged forward and punched Timmy square in the face. "Suck your what bitch?" Joe Joe rushed low grabbing one of Timmy's legs and taking him to the ground.

"Get the fuck off me," Timmy yelled out as he reached up trying to block the stampede of punches that Joe Joe had been landing on his face.

"Fuck you Pussy!" Joe Joe yelled as he stood to his feet and began stomping and kicking Timmy in his head.

"Stop! Stop!" Mrs. Jones yelled as she ran towards the fight.

X heard his mom's voice and quickly wrestled Joe Joe off of Timmy.

"Bitch!" Joe Joe says between grinding teeth as he gets one last stomp off while X pulls him away.

"You better stop it right now Joseph Blakely!" Erupts Mrs. Jones towards Joe Joe as she stands between him and Timmy.

Joe Joe just stared at Mrs. Jones for a moment gathering his self. "I'm sorry Mrs. Jones." Smirking as he came back to reality just as fast as he zoned out. Responding to Mrs. Jones's comment. "I know he didn't touch me, but he was talking to me greasy and disrespectful."

Knowing she had Joe Joe right where she wanted him. "So, you mean to tell me that you didn't say anything disrespectful to provoke what went on between you and C?"

"You're right Mrs. Jones. I may have provoked it a little." Giving up the verbal game.

"It doesn't matter that I'm right. All that matters is that you and C get right because all this fighting and carrying on is pure foolishness. Because both of ya'll keep hanging with Xavier and that's just too close for comfort if you ask me. I swear ya'll ain't going to be happy until someone gets seriously hurt or ki..." Mrs. Jones busts out into tears when she thinks of the possible severity of their actions.

"I'm over it Mrs. Jones, I promise." Confirms Joe Joe as he watches X embrace his mom.

"Nothing is going to happen to anyone ma. They just had a macho man match, and it's over, as you always say when me and C get into it."

Joe Joe shrugged his shoulders. "It wasn't that big of a deal. We just disagreed. I'm really over it."

"And I'm going to talk to my nephew today because this shit has got to stop!" Mrs. Jones spoke sharply with hurt and not anger, and both X and Joe Joe knew it.

This was X's first time hearing his mom cuss since she got saved so he knew she was serious. "Mom let's put all this behind us this morning and go get your stuff."

Wiping the tears from her face. "I love you knuckleheads. And I'm going to pray that Jesus touches all of your hearts to let in some love for your brothers next to you. And that you guys stop displaying so much hate for people living where you live. Going through the same type of problems that you go through. Ya'll have to realize that life is more important than your individual issues."

They both answer, "Yes ma'am."

CHAPTER 11

After about twenty minutes of driving, C finally arrived at his three, bedroom plush home in Newton Falls. Upon entering his house, he can see his wife Bernadette vacuuming and singing along with her R&B music. "Hey, baby." C said in a dull tone.

"What's the matter, baby?" Bernadette asked in concern.

Staring at his wife with wondrous eyes C responds. "Nothing now that I'm home with my fine ass wife." Wrapping his arms around her from the back, he laid a soft kiss on the side of her neck. "So, where's my little angel?"

Sarcastically. "Oh, your little angel? Well, our little monster wouldn't stop jumping around out here. So, I made her go back into her room to play while I clean up." Putting her hand on her hip. "She must not have heard your music when you pulled up or she would've already been out here. And you know that." Wrapping up the vacuuming cleaner. "So, baby… What's bothering you?"

C let out a sigh before answering. "Man… why did I have to go upside Lil Joe Joe's head this morning?"

Taken aback. "Hold up! Are you talking about X's little friend?"

"Yeah. I'm talking about that little ungrateful motherfucker. He called his self, talking greasy to me cause, he can't get no dope, and I won't serve him."

Confused. "So, what? He supposed to be a fiend now?"

Letting out a laugh. "Nah. Not a fiend, but a hustler. He wanted me to sell him a double-up so he could keep making sales. When I refused to serve him like I always do. This little punk came out of his mouth and called me a bitch!" Mocking Joe Joe's posture. "With his chest sticking out like he was big or something."

Bernadette can't help but smile as she admires her husband's brawn, while he demonstrates. "So be honest... He didn't like your octopus arm speech?" Knowing her husband all too well.

Laughing as he talks. "I guess you can say that. But he could've just said that and walked away. Instead, he made me have to - embarrass him." Getting more serious. "And the crazy part of it all is, I really like this little nigga."

"You don't say." Jokingly.

"Nah I'm not shy truthin. I really do." Trying to think of the perfect way to explain. "Like I know of real-life incidents that my little cousin would've probably got his head taken off if it weren't for Joe Joe. And, truth be told, he's X's friend not mine anyways. And for X, I think he's absolutely right for the team. I know he bad as hell, but he got all the reason in the world. His mom's a dope fiend, his dad's been in prison since he was five, and his big brother, the only nigga that ever really looked out for him just got murdered, what... three years ago. All that boy knows is pain." Shaking off his thoughts of himself. "That's why I can see past the outburst. All I knew was pain. Until I met you."

Grasping his fact. "Well baby, I just pray that you two can get over all this and move on without further incident." Grabbing C's shirt and pulling him closer as she speaks. "Ya'll are literally all X has in his corner. And he needs both of ya'll." Kissing him with a couple of soft smooches. "And you're most definitely all we got. So, I can't have anything happening to you out here over no dumb shit."

"Daddy!" C's daughter Essence yells as she runs into the room. "Daddy!" Arms wide open.

C picked Essence up and kissed both her cheeks and gave her a big hug. "How's daddy's little angel this morning?"

With the biggest smile. "Good daddy." Shaking C's leg when he puts her down. "Daddy, Daddy! Guess what I did today." Not really pausing long enough to get a response. "Mommy let me help her with the dishes."

"Oh snap! Look at daddy's big girl doing big girl chores." Lifting her chin. "What are you thirteen?"

Shaking his leg harder. "Daddy you know I'm five."

"Oh yeah. I be forgetting sometimes because you be such a big girl. So, what did you do? Wash or rinse?"

"She let me rinse. She said she was doing the hard part, but it didn't look too hard to me. And she said I did so good, she's gonna take me to the ice cream place. And she said I can get any kind I want."

"Oh, did she now? And I bet you want cookies n' cream ice cream huh?" Hinting on to his favorite flavor.

"I just might. It all depends on what I get in return." Pointing in Essence's direction. "She gave me a lot of help today. And what are you willing to do for your ice cream?" Giving C a wink of the eye. "I think it's only fair that you earn yours. I mean Essence had to earn hers." Signaling her eye contact with her daughter. "Don't you think that would be fair honey?"

Essence in full agreement. "Yes, mommy!"

C chimes in on their conspiracy. "So, I get it. Daddy gotta do some big boy chores to get some ice cream." Throwing a wink back.

Leaning in and landing another smooch. "Aww! Look who gets it." Bernadette swiftly walks off into the bedroom and closes the door.

"Hey Baby girl. You want daddy to make you some popcorn and put you on a movie?" Trying to bide her time.

"Yeah, Daddy! Movie time!" Essence shouted as she jumped up and down in a circle.

"Well I'm gonna start the popcorn and you go pick any movie you wanna watch." After getting her settled C went into the bedroom to join his wife.

Bernadette was lying across the bed wearing silky red lingerie. Her slow music playing. "I hope you like it."

"Like it?" Feeling himself growing in his pants. "I love it. You should let me go take a shower real quick."

"You should come over here with me and get dirty before you go take your shower." Bernadette laid back on her pillows and pulled her panties to the side exposing her freshly shaved, juicy lips. "I think she's been waiting for you to come home long enough."

Without hesitating, C dove face first into her welcoming quim. Sucking and licking on her clit as she quivers in pleasure.

"Oh, Carl! You're gonna make me cum so much! Oh, baby... I can't hold it!" Bernadette's love juices came rushing out of her like lava from an erupting volcano.

"Is this what she wanted?" Carl whispered to her. Lifting himself to come out of his clothes.

"Oh yes. This is what she needed." Taking C's swollen penis in.

C stroked her slow to the rhythm of the music. Deeper and deeper, until he felt himself about to explode. "Oh my God baby I can't take it. Your pussy feels so good to me."

Feeling him reaching his point. "Just a little bit more baby! I'm about to cum again too! I want to cum with you!"

C began to stroke her vigorously until they both began to tremble in orgasmic pleasure. "Oh shit! He moaned out. After he was done C rolled over out of breath and reflected on the moment they just had. After getting his marbles together he reached over and grabbed a rolled cigar out of his pants.

Bernadette realizing what C has in his hand. "C'mon baby. You know I don't like you smoking in here."

"Baby, I'm sorry. But after that good shit, I need to smoke." Slapping her on her butt, before lighting his blunt.

"Do you think you'll ever quit?" Asking in a concerned voice.

"Quit what? Quit smoking? Where is this coming from?"

"Not smoking. But hustling."

Shaking his head vexed. "Are we really about to do this right now? I mean two seconds, later? Really?"

"Baby I'm sorry. I'm not asking to be mad and argue. I just be so worried about you out there and I don't want anything to

54

happen to you." Taking a deep breath. "And it ain't like I can just pop up on you out there and see you when I want to."

Cutting her off mid-sentence. "And you already know why. I can't risk nobody doing anything to ya'll because of me."

I'm just saying this is hard for me. While you're in Warren doing what you do, I'm right here with our daughter praying that God lets my husband make it home in good health. Then like today, you're always having to put your hands on somebody. What if…" She pauses embracing the severity of her words. "What if one-day things don't go in your favor?" Bernadette turns to hide her tears from C.

Pulling her back to him. "Baby I'm good out here. I keep telling you I don't be in the type of drama you got to worry about. You don't see me ducked off at war. We are good. I want to quit too. But our lifestyle ain't cheap. So, I do what I got to do for us."

Pushing him away. "For us? It's really hard to see that when every time I look up it's just me and Essence here." Regaining her composer. "Do you know that sometimes I sit here and pretend that you're dead and you're not ever coming home? I guess I'm just taking your advice and…"

Letting out an uncomfortable chuckle. "I wasn't talking about planning my funeral to prepare for the worst. Baby look, I'm sorry for worrying you. But I promise I'm not trying to let anything happen to me. I already died once and got another chance. I don't think I'm lucky enough to get that same deal again. Honestly, I don't want that deal again." Referring to the day he lost his parents. "Now you know I didn't choose this life. It chose me. If you really want me to get out of it, just say the word. Now I'm not saying it'll be an overnight change, but it will definitely be a change."

"Baby, I said those vows knowing exactly who you were. And I meant every word. I think I've done a hell of a job at being by your side through a whole life of thick times. All I'm saying is it's hard. If you really can't quit, then I guess all I can do is continue to pray for you and support you. I love you, baby. With my whole life."

"I love you too." C got up and went into the bathroom to take his shower. "And I understand where you coming from."

When C came back into the room Bernadette points to his phone that she placed on the charger. "Your phone was ringing while you were in there."

"Did you answer it?"

With an attitude. "Do I ever answer your phone?"

C grabs his phone and dials the last number back, which happened to be Sam. His weed contact. "What's the business fam?" C asked after Sam answers.

"Shit. What it always is. Prosperous. How you looking on your side?" Sam asked.

"I'm running low on the dro." Peeking out the blinds. "I'm probably going to have to get up with you A.S.A.P. on that."

"Cool. Cool. I got about ten pounds left. How many you want?"

Calculating his funds. "Shit... I'll take like five of them. And if you still got that good fluffy shit. I'll take an eight-piece of that."

Confirming the deal. "You're in luck cause all I got is nine left and you know I'm smoking one. So, give me twelve thousand for the dro and give me seven thousand for the fluff." Setting the bait.

"I feel like you are forcing me to spend all my money with you with these good ass deals." C said jokingly.

Cocky. "And what's wrong with that?" Singing. "I'm a hustler. I'm a, I'm a hustler."

"Alright hustler. Meet me around my place in forty-five minutes."

"O.k. I'll see you there."

After hanging up the phone C turned to Bernadette. "Hey baby, can you grab me twenty-thousand out of the safe?"

"Which safe? You know it's three of them in there."

"X's safe. I'm about to get some weed." C texted X to let him know he's on his way to pick him up.

Bernadette retrieves the money for C and plants one more soft kiss on his lips. "Be careful out there baby."

"I will." C tucks the money then goes into the living room to speak to Essence. "Bye, my Angel. Daddy got to run." Taking one more look at both his ladies before leaving. "I love ya'll."

CHAPTER 12

Waiting on C's arrival, X looks at Joe Joe who is sitting on the step behind him. "Look, Bro, my mom is right. You and C are gonna have to drop this shit for me, cause it's really uncomfortable having ya'll right back around each other."

"So, what? You want me to leave? Cause the way it looks to me is you and your mom only coming at me about this shit. Ain't nobody gonna say a word to C." Angrily. "I'm saying. I know that's your cousin and all but everybody ain't gonna just be letting him put his hands on them. Somebody gonna let him have it. Mark my words."

Standing to his feet. "So, what are you saying nigga? You wanna kill my cousin?"

Rising up as well. "What I'm saying is if it were anybody else you would've had my back a hundred grand. But since it was Lord C, now you wanna fight me cause I'm mad about it." Bumping past X to get down the steps. "And you already know how I get down. If it were anyone else, I'd be at they ass. But I ain't about to do shit to C. For the sake of you being my brother from another. But you better let that nigga know it ain't gonna be no next time." They can hear C's music in the distance approaching. "That sounds like that nigga right there. Let's see if the cat gets your tongue when it comes time to say something to him."

"What the fuck ever nigga. You just be cool." Looking down the street to see C turning onto his street.

When C pulls up, he turns his music off before hopping out. "I hope you're ready because we got about fifteen minutes before we gotta meet Sam."

"So, what, we gotta meet him at the doghouse?" Questioned X.

With an attitude. "Where else we gonna meet him at?"

X, rubbing his hands together nervously. "Well, I'm ready to roll. But before we go, I'm going to need ya'll to squash ya'lls beef."

Waving X off. "Man, don't nobody got beef with your homie. If we had beef, I wouldn't be standing here all calm talking to you while he's standing here. I'd be trying to get at his ass." C turned his attention towards Joe Joe. "So, what? You wanna go to war with me about this morning? If you do, I can understand, but I'm willing to keep it moving on the whole situation. I mean anyways... What I look like going to war with my right-hand man's, right-hand man?" Reaching his hand out to Joe Joe.

Joe Joe looked at C's hand but didn't grab it. "Man.... Ain't nobody trying to go to war with you, but I ain't gonna act like that shit just cool with me. I don't give a fuck who it is or how much money a nigga got. Everybody knows Joe Joe gonna shoot if a nigga tries to harm me."

Letting out a chuckle. "And that's what I like about you. You're little as fuck and you don't take shit from nobody. But one thing you're gonna have to learn is, everybody ain't gonna take your shit neither. Cause I'm a man before I'm anything. So, when you go swinging your cojones around like your top dog and calling me bitches, then I'm gonna treat you as such and show you what being a man is about."

"What the fuck you talking about? I pay my own bills! Buy my own clothes! Feed myself! I don't ask nobody for no handouts ever. If I can't buy it. Then I can't try it." Pounding his hands together as he talks.

"And just because you got the cash. Don't mean I gotta serve your ass." Displaying his smugness. "On the real, I won't even sell X dope and he's older than you."

"Well, I'm not X. And that's how I get down."

"I don't have no problem with that. But it's not gonna change how I move." Looking stern. "My advice to you is to start buying bigger and stacking your dope instead of your money. So, when the drought comes around, you'll be the only one with dope and you can raise your price. But you gotta stop thinking I owe you any more than that in the game." Turning his attention to X. "Now that everybody has kissed and made up can we get the fuck out of here? Talking about me not serving this nigga. Sam ain't gonna serve me shit if I keep him waiting." Tapping his watch. "Time is money."

Joe Joe gives X a handshake. "Don't forget to holler at me when you get right."

"I won't" Getting in the car. "That shit was going to bother me all day."

"You be stressing all the wrong shit, little cuz." Mashing the gas. "All I'm stressing right now is getting this pack and feeding my dogs."

"Why you got so many dogs anyways?"

"Cheap labor." C declared. "All I do is feed them and pet them every day. And in return, they dedicate their lives to watching over my drugs. And more important… they all are guaranteed to be one hundred percent loyal, one hundred percent of the time. If a nigga can find my shit and get it out of the house with all eight of my dogs on guard, then he deserves to have it."

Realizing the method to C's madness. "I never thought of it like that. I guess that's pretty genius. Free security."

"Exactly! And speaking of loyal security. You better keep your eyes open on your boy. That nigga not built like you. He good when he on top and when he not I think anybody can get it. Including you."

"Nah, for real. We have been in some real drama before, and he never folded on me." X corrected.

"Was ya'll losing?" C asked opening up his point to be proven.

"We never lose cuz." Cocky.

"And that's my whole point. As long as things are working in his favor, he's good. As soon as something doesn't go his way, anything and anybody becomes a bargaining chip to get what he wants." Speaking humbly. "I could be wrong, but it won't hurt to just take heed to the words that are coming out of my mouth."

"I ain't gonna lie. You right, but he doesn't ever come at me like that. It's always me and him against the world." Trying to explain how he interprets the situation.

"That's probably because you already whooped his ass before, and he knows you're not having it. Like today for instance. He knows that I have not and will not serve him and that never bothered him any other time. As long as his connect was good. But as soon as his connect got a little shaky he wants to lash out at me for not serving him."

"I feel what you're saying but I don't know... I just..." Fumbling over his words. "I guess I know his whole life and I be feeling his anger. And I kind of understand why he be acting out sometimes. His life has been a nightmare. At the end of the day, I think he knows that I'm the only one in his corner a hundred grand. And I know he can be extreme at times. But knowing where he comes from, I've learned to accept it."

Pulling into his driveway. "Well, however, you've excepted him. Your boys a snake in the grass and I hope you see that before you get bit." C looked in his rearview mirror to see Sam pulling in behind him. "Hey X umm. Why don't you..."

Cutting C off. "I got you. I'll be right back. Do you want some Dutch's or something from the store?"

"Yeah, just give me like fifteen minutes before you come back so I can handle this."

"Alright." C got out of the car and X climbed across to the driver's seat. "What's up Smokey Sam!"

"What's good with ya'll two ballers?" Sam said holding two large duffle bags.

"What ain't good with us?" C said arrogantly. "Let's go in the back and handle this."

Sam followed C through his gate, and onto an enclosed patio. "So, you said you wanted five of the dro and eight of the fluff?" Unzipping the bags and setting them on the table.

"Everything weighed out?" Taking two ounces of each and placing them on the scale. "Twenty-nine a piece."

Assuredly. "And those bags only weigh point eight so you're winning a gram every five. You know my math is always on point. Now how bout yours?" Sam waved his hand over the table like a magician.

C sat his duffle bag on the table and exposed his money. "You know I stay on point like a needle."

"Everything been counted?" Sam asked mocking C.

"Twice at my house and a third time when you get it home." Smugly. "What… We been doing this for seven years now? Never been a dollar or a gram short. If anything, it's been extra dollars and extra grams. I ain't never said it but I really appreciate the loyalty and realness you've shown me since I came home. I can't say the same for all these fuck niggas around here." Extending his hand.

"Shit… Thank you for coming home the same nigga since the sandbox." Receiving C's gesture. "I gotta roll. I got like four more places to be five minutes ago." On the way back to his car Sam motions towards the dogs in the cages. "What's up with some puppies?"

'I'm still debating which one of my males I'm going to use. My black girl should be going in heat in about a month. But you know as soon as I get shit in motion, you're going to be the first to know."

Getting in his car. "How much you going to hit me for a boy?"

C gripping his chin. "I don't know, but it ain't going to be a lot. Shit if you get some more of that fluff; We might be able to work out something real sweet."

"Well till we meet again my brother from another." Saluting C before backing out of the driveway.

Hearing his music roaring closer. "This nigga banging my shit like he me?" Watching X pull up and get out of the car. "That's what I sound like pulling up on ya'll?"

"Hell yeah. Like Godzilla! I didn't want to come back too fast, so I slid the block a little. How'd everything turn out? We back a go?"

"You already know, everything's everything." Leading the way back towards the patio. "I got two of each for you to start with."

X rubbing his hands together in excitement. "Same ticket?"

Looking back at X. "What, you want me to raise it?"

Laughing off his comment. "Nah. You said if shit went your way you might drop the price some."

Remembering. "Damn! I did say that, didn't I? Well, take twenty-five off each one. A deal's a deal. Business ain't shit if you can't take a nigga's word for nothing."

"Thanks, man. That boost is about to make such a big difference." Exuberating his appreciation.

"Well if it makes so much a difference. How about you feed the outside dogs, while I take care of the inside dogs." Showing a smile from ear to ear.

"You know I got you on that even without a discount."

CHAPTER 13

"Mommy, why do people have bad dreams?" Asked Essence.

"I can't really say, baby. Every person's different. Maybe they saw something scary before they went to sleep, and it makes them have a nightmare." Bernadette answered thoughtfully.

Shaking her head in disagreement. "No not a nightmare mommy. I'm talking about a bad dream. Daddy told me that nightmares have monsters and bad dreams have real people."

In awe. "Daddy said that, did he? Way to go daddy." Bernadette mumbles under her breath. "Well, some people say that when you have a bad dream about someone close to you, it's God's way of warning you to watch out for that person. Did you ask me that because you've been having bad dreams about someone close to you?"

"I keep having a dream that someone shoots daddy. And every time I see him fall, I wake up, and I be scared." Her innocence showing in her face. "Mommy. I don't want nobody to shoot daddy."

Ahh baby, don't worry. Daddy's going to be alright." Grabbing her chin to look her in the eyes. "Now you listen to me ok. Next time you have a bad dream about daddy, I want you to pray to God that he watches over daddy and protects him from harm. And when you do, God will make sure daddy's okay."

"Okay, mommy."

The phone began to ring. Bernadette can see that it is her friend Sharon before she picks up. "Hello!"

"Don't hello me Bern. Spit it out." Sharon demanded.

"I didn't get to tell him," Bernadette said sadly.

"Why what happened?" interrogated Sharon.

"Hold on a sec." Bernadette looked towards Essence. "Hey baby, how about you go and get yourself dressed, so when I get off the phone I can take you to get your ice cream." Watching her run down the hallway, she continued to answer Sharon. "Man, he came in going off about an altercation he had earlier this morning. And I don't know. When he got done talking about it, the mood was lost, and I didn't feel like it was the right time to tell him."

"It's never going to seem like the right time Bern. You're just going to have to tell that man that you're having his baby. It ain't like he's some random guy you're dating. He's your husband."

"I know. I know. It's just that I want at least the setting to be happy when I tell him." Rubbing her stomach.

I understand all that, but girl… how happy do you think he's going to be when he walks into a beach ball for a stomach on his wife one day, and you never said a word?"

"I guess you're right. I'm going to tell him, girl. I ain't even going to lie. I'm borderline scared. I don't know why. I mean he was so happy when I told him I was pregnant with Essence."

"The fear is all in your head girl. You know how much C loves you." Confirmed Sharon.

"I know. But what if he says he's not ready for another kid right now."

"Then that's when you tell him he shouldn't have had so much fun while he was up in that." They both let out a laugh. "No pun intended, but it's a little late to not be ready."

"Girl, you are so crazy! I promise I'm going to tell him."

"Well make sure you call and let me know what he says. And good luck."

"Thank you and I will. Bye girl."

"Goodbye"

After hanging up the phone, Bernadette just sat on the couch thinking about how much she and C have been through. And how she would probably be dead if it weren't for her savior, her hero, her husband. She fell into a deep daydream.

"Drop me off over my mom's house until you're done," Bernadette said to Tony as she leaned her seat back.

"What the fuck you mean? Drop you off over your mom's house?" In a mocking voice. "You're taking your ass home," Tony said, denying her request.

Looking at Tony angrily. "I'm tired of sitting in the house by myself while you run the streets with your homeboys."

Speaking with disgust. "Bitch, I see you're not going to be happy until I go upside your motherfucking head!"

Closing her eyes as she shouts back. "If you put your hands on me. I swear to God…"

Tony snatched Bernadette by her hair. "You swear to God what bitch?"

The car came to a stop and Bernadette slapped Tony to free herself before jumping out. "I hate you! Leave me alone!" She screamed.

Tony jumped out also and rushed Bernadette. Grabbing her by her throat and forcing her to the ground. "Bitch I told you what was going to happen. You just didn't want to listen." Squeezing tighter. "Now I'm about to choke the life out of you!"

Barely holding on. "Please stop." In a faint voice.

Snatching her back up to her feet. "Get your ass the fuck back in the car!" Tony opened the passenger door and slammed her inside.

"Get the fuck off of me Tony!" Snatching away.

Furious, Tony began wailing on Bernadette who just balled up in the fetal position trying to block his blows. "I swear your gonna make me kill your stupid ass!"

Right when she thought to herself. This would never end. A set of built arms came out of nowhere grabbing Tony by his neck and pulling him back off of her. "You like to beat women? Huh, motherfucker." C threw Tony to the ground before pulling out his pistol. Before Tony could get back to his feet C grabbed him up by his shirt and began to beat him across his face with the but of his gun. "I swear to God I should fucking kill your ass. If I catch you anywhere near her again, you're dead! Do you hear me? Your dead!" Releasing Tony's limp body C walked over to

Bernadette and offered his hand to help her out of the car. "Are you okay?"

"Yes. But my clothes." Bernadette looked down at her shirt which was hanging on to her by a thread. Exposing her bra. "Can you please take me to change my clothes?"

C showed a soft smile. "Sure." Opening her door. "I'll run you by my place and get you a shirt since it's right around the corner." Looking at her with empathy. "If that's cool with you?"

"I just want to get away from here. Please." Looking at Tony squirming, coming to. Then looking in the visor mirror at her face. "You finally got yours." Under her breath.

Getting in and noticing Bernadette examining herself. "You still look beautiful. I'm going to take care of you just right. Lord knows I done had my share of bumps and bruises."

Blushing. "Thank you. I really am sorry that I got you in all this."

"I'm sorry you didn't get me into this a long time ago. That nigga shouldn't be putting his hands on you period." Hitting his hand on the steering wheel. "I should've bodied his ass." Pulling up in his driveway. "And you don't owe me thanks. I did what that nigga deserved me to do. Sometimes God works through the people around you. That's why he made me pull up right when I did." Motioning her to get out. "Let's get you cleaned up."

Bernadette followed close behind C into the house. "You're not going to get in trouble with your girlfriend for having me in here are you?"

Laughing as if it were a big joke. "I don't have a girlfriend to get in trouble by. Let me get you some stuff to get comfy." Disappearing down the hallway before reappearing with fresh towels and a t-shirt and basketball shorts. "The shorts might fit a little big, but they got drawstrings to tighten them."

Taking the items from C. "Thank you so much. I really don't know what I'd do without you right now."

"Then hang on to me." Smiling. "The bathroom is right down that way."

After she got changed Bernadette walked into the room where C had been smoking a blunt and listening to some music and changed his CD to some slow music. "So, what do you think?" Running her hands down her side to display herself.

C looked up to see Bernadette's smooth, thick, chocolate thighs coming from under the tee. Taking a gulp. "I think, that I've never seen that shirt look so good before."

Bernadette straddled C, staring him deep into his eyes before kissing him softly.

"Mommy, mommy I'm ready!" Essence brought Bernadette back to reality.

"Girl, if you don't go back in there and put on some real clothes." Noticing she had on her make-believe, dress-up clothes.

"But mommy… I want to be a princess today."

"Well go put on your glitter outfit that you said makes you feel like a princess." After watching Essence go back into the room she fell into another daydream.

The news reporters' voice echoes the room. "And in our breaking news report for today. The identity of the body that was found in a burning car on four twenty-two early last week, has been identified to be a Warren Ohio resident named Anthony Brodel. After further autopsy reports, it has been determined that Brodel had been shot three times in the head before being placed in the trunk of his car and being set ablaze. No information on the suspect has been given. If you or someone you know has any information that could lead police to a possible suspect call the number displayed on your screen."

"Oh, Tony." Bernadette stared at the T.V. blankly. Remembering the conversation, she had with C a week prior. How she said she will never feel safe with Tony walking around the same streets she did. How she told C that she feared for his safety as well. She got the chills when she pictured the coldness on his face that she somehow missed in the moment. The exact words he said when he told her he wouldn't rest until she felt safe again. And just how much she thought to herself that she wanted C to take care of Tony. C never told her that he was responsible for what happened to Tony, and she never asked. But deep inside she always knew to herself that no one in the city was brave enough to step to Tony. Except for her knight in shining armor.

Once again Essence voice brought Bernadette back to attention. "Mommy are you okay? You were just staring in the sky."

"Yeah, baby. Mommy just got a lot on her mind right now. That's all."

"Daddy always says if I got something on my mind, I can talk to him about anything. Maybe you should talk to daddy, mommy." Not even knowing the level of wisdom in her words.

Nodding in agreement. "You know what? I think your right baby. I'm going to talk to daddy about it." Rubbing her stomach. "That's a great idea."

CHAPTER 14

Putting his car into drive, C looks over at X who is attempting to blow smoke rings. "Thanks again for helping me with the dogs."

As if he didn't hear C. "Man, I almost had one!"

"What the fuck X?" Snapped C.

Looking like a kid caught. "What? Why you flipping?"

Speaking firm. "So, you didn't just hear me thanking you for your help?

"Yeah I heard you. Damn! I had a mouth full of smoke and I was concentrating."

"Man, you just said I almost had one. So, you very easily could've said you're welcome, no problem, anytime. Something to say that you acknowledge what the fuck I'm saying to you." Raising his voice.

"My Bad. I guess I was just zoned out. I really wasn't trying to ignore you. But I always be zoning out. So, why you so mad this time?"

"I ain't mad. I just ain't on bullshit. You are doing some real juvenile type shit sometimes."

"And like I said. Been doing that. So why trip?" Giving C the eye. "So, are you going to tell me what's bothering you or are you just going to keep acting like I'm bothering you?"

"You right little cuz. I was thinking about some shit Bernadette was talking about this morning, and it got me feeling some type of way. It ain't shit though." Trying to minimize the situation.

"Contraire mon frère. It gotta be big for you to be snapping off like that. What's good big cuz? What? She talking about leaving you?"

Taking a deep breath. "More like me leaving her. She said she thinks I'm going to end up dead."

"Well, in all honesty, we're all going to end up dead. What's important is what we do with the time we have, to make it worth living."

"And that's pretty much where she's coming from. She wants me to stop hustling." Looking baffled. "Can you imagine me not hustling?"

"Honestly I couldn't. You have been hustling since you got home. And it just seems like your throne in life. But I'm your little cousin and she's your wife. So, we're not going to see you the same way. And you got to expect her to want you more to herself." Pausing briefly. "Be real with yourself. If she just wanted you to keep hustling to bring in the dough and never cared about what happens to you while you're out there. You would have to question her sincerity for ya'lls whole relationship. The reason she wants you to quit just says to me that she cares about you more than the money, and that means you have to really decide between your wife and your street life."

"So, what you saying? You think I should call it quits in the streets?"

"I think you should take at least a weekend off and spend it with your wife and let that time with her to be your deciding factor."

Nodding in agreement. "I think you might be on to something. When I get to the house, I'm going to reserve a room in Cleveland. Just so we can be in a whole other atmosphere."

"That's going to be dope." There was a silence in the car for a few seconds and X had a thought. "I know this is totally off subject, but I want to ask you something?"

Not knowing where X was heading. "Shoot."

"I don't know why, but I been wondering. And you're like the only person I can ask. But... How does it feel to kill someone?"

Looking at X in awe. "What? Are you planning on killing someone?"

"Nah. I just be thinking to myself sometimes, like... would I have the balls to pull the trigger or would I be too scared to? And if I did, would I go crazy from the guilt."

C turned into X's driveway. "Man." Letting out a sigh. "I don't really know how to say it. I mean when I killed Red and Saint, I felt relieved. I swear I walked around that jail with my head held high and a smile on my face because I did that shit for my parents and I knew they deserved to die." Wiping his face down. "Now on the other hand. There were dudes in there that killed people on some gang shit and they were in there crying all the time about how they just wanted to go home. How they were sorry for what they had done. And how they just wanted to change their lives. So, I guess at the end of the day it all depends on your conscience and how it perceives right and wrong."

"I can feel that. So how did you feel after Bernadette's old dude?"

Taken aback. "Where the fuck you get that I killed that nigga?"

"Everybody in the streets say you killed that nigga."

"Well, I ain't saying I did. So, with that being said, if I did kill him. I probably would've felt good about that too. Being that he was beating on my future wife at the time."

"Do you think that she believes you killed him?"

"I don't know what she believes. I just know she never asked me, and when the police asked her if she knew who might've done it her answer was no. But shit, she might just be holding it in like you been all this time." Speaking under his breath. "Thinking ya'll know something." C watched as the police cruised slowly by the house, looking in their direction. "Alright. Let's go into the house before this motherfucker comes back to ask me some questions too."

As soon as they entered the house they both plopped down on opposite ends of the couch. "Hey C. Do you ever wonder how long you're going to live?"

C shaking his head. "Damn! You're really on a death kick today, ain't you?"

X realizing his question might've struck a nerve. Quickly explains. "It ain't that I'm on a death kick. I have just been thinking about all the people our age that be dying around here.

And it just seems like nobody grows old anymore. Shit makes you wonder."

"Well, you know what the Bible says. Ask and you shall receive. Seek and you shall find. Knock and the door will be open. You just keep looking for answers and God's going to give you all the answers you need." Laughing as he notices his aunt pulling up outside. "Shit if you don't go put that stank ass weed up before my auntie gets in here you might get all your questions answered sooner than you think."

Hopping up from the couch. "Oh shit! This shit is reeking!" Spraying air freshener around the house. "I ain't trying to experience a painful death."

Ms. Carol enters the house right after X closes his bedroom door. "Hey, honey! How's my favorite nephew doing today?"

"I'm your only nephew Auntie." Standing to his feet to greet her with a hug. "But other than a little early morning drama with Joe Joe, my day's been going pretty good. How's your day going?"

"Forget my day. Why you put your hands on that boy?"

"I ain't even going to lie to you, Auntie. He asked me to sell him something and I refused him business. And next thing I know I'm all sorts of bitches." Covering his mouth. "Oops! I'm sorry. But I was all kinds of BS. And I even tried to warn him. But after he refused to take heed to my warnings I had to do what I had to do. I bet every time he sees that fat lip he's going to think twice about how he talks to people."

"You remind me so much of your father. From the way you look, down to the way you act. I'm sitting here listening to you explain to me what happened and all I can see is your dad talking to me. So, I guess it's okay for you to sell drugs in our neighborhood because you're a little older than Joe Joe?"

"A little older? Joe Joe's like thirteen or fourteen years old and I'm twenty-five." As if that were an intelligent answer.

"So once again. Does that give you the okay to do what you do?" Poking C stiffly in the chest as she speaks.

Finding no justification. "No, ma'am. But Auntie. What I was saying by him being too young is he still got a whole life ahead of him to be whatever he chooses. When me on the other hand, I got out of prison with two murder charges. I didn't have a choice but to turn to our family business for money."

"I totally despise the way you refer to your street dealings as our family business. We have men in our family that's known for a lot more respectable things and I think it's about time that you recognize and acknowledge that." Trying to hold back her tears. "Now I empathize with your story. God knows I do. But I refuse to sit back quietly and watch you run amuck with your life while my brother rolls over in his grave because you chose to grow up and put on the exact shoes he tried to hide from you for so long. It was wrong when he did it and he lost his life behind it. And it's just as wrong with you doing it knowing this life is the reason you have to live without parents. And now you want to volunteer your life to it. I pray God doesn't make your kid have to relive your reality before someone finally gets the picture. But that's all I can do is pray. It's up to you to want better for yourself and your family."

Seeing the pain in her tears. "I'm sorry Auntie. I wasn't trying to upset you."

"Don't be sorry to me. You need to be sorry to that beautiful wife of yours and that sweet innocent daughter you two made. You don't think your daughter is ever going to put together the fact that her father is a drug dealer?" Not giving him the chance to respond. "And what are you going to tell her when she's old enough to date and she falls for a drug dealer like yourself to be her boyfriend?"

"What else can I tell her? I'm going to tell her the truth."

"And what is that exactly?"

The truth is that the life I been living may be profitable but it's not happy. And that life is too short to not be happy. At the same time, I'm going to warn her of all the traps and dangers that come with it. After that, all I can do is pray for her as you pray for me. But for right now, I got to get this money."

74

"Well, I'm glad that you got it all mapped out. And I hope everything goes exactly as you plan it to. But meanwhile, just think of how much easier it'll be if you really would change your life and you tell her that she's the reason. I think that would be the impact a great father wants to have on his child. Now I know you're not going to be a saint overnight, but at least try to dedicate some quality time to spend with your family and don't forget to pray. And I think God will do the rest. That's one thing about God. He always knows what we need to do in situations even when we don't."

"Have you been talking to X or something? Because I swear he told me pretty much the same thing earlier."

"Or maybe that's God trying to make you get the message." Displaying a big smile.

Coming to a decision. "Well, Auntie. I think I'm going to listen to you and X and take some time off to spend with my family. And to be honest. I have been wanting to quit for a while now. I just don't know what to do if I don't do this."

"Put your past behind you nephew and live. Just live."

CHAPTER 15

C headed to Mr. Lupino's but the whole way there all he could think about was his conversation with his aunt. As soon as he enters the store, he is greeted by Mr. Lupino's smile. "What you know old man?"

Mr. Lupino quickly remarked back. "It would be a shorter list if I tell you what I don't know. You know I know everything. Let me walk you downstairs. Nephew just called right before you pulled up and said he'd be here in ten minutes.

"I know I've been down here like a thousand times before, but it still amazes me how it looks every time I come down here. C says as he looks around. "I mean, you just don't picture this being under the store.

Mr. Lupino looked over at the monitor where he could see Nephew pulling up. "Go ahead and make yourself a drink or something. I'm going to go upstairs and let Nephew in."

C cracked open a beer and while he was pouring his self a shot of Gin, he hears Mr. Lupino and Nephew coming down the steps. "Do either of you want a shot while I'm pouring mine?"

"I thought you're supposed to say hi before you offer people drinks and shit. I could be wrong but that's just what I thought." Laughing as he shakes C's hand.

"My bad man. I got a lot on my mind. Got me acting a little off I guess. But what you been up to?"

"You know me. Living the dream. But I'm going to take your offer on that drink." Patting C on the shoulder. "Friends don't let friends drink alone under stress."

"I'm good though. It's just life. And you know the only option other than living your life is not living and that don't sound like an option that I'm interested in." Directing his attention to Mr. Lupino. "And will you be having a drink with us today sir?"

Waving C off. "I'm going to let ya'll boys drink it up tonight. If this old man has a drink right now, I'm closing the store for the rest of the day."

Nephew blurts out. "You must be remembering last time you got drunk and started giving kids all the snacks out the store for free. You know what they say. A drunk person is an honest person. You're honestly just a good guy Unc."

"Well, this good guy is not trying to bankrupt the store today." Mr. Lupino gave a grin.

Nephew raised his glass to make a toast. "C it's been a long time coming for both of us. And Unc told us it wouldn't be easy, but somehow, we always made it look easy. So, with that being said. To us! Lifelong partners, friends, and brothers. Salute!"

Tapping his glass to Nephews. "I'll drink to that!" After swallowing his shot and chasing it down with some beer C let out a sigh. "Aye for real. There's something I've got to talk to both of ya'll about." Noticing he had their full attention. "I've been doing a lot of thinking lately and I've come to the conclusion that I need to step away from the game. I don't know if it's going to be permanent, but what I do know is it's going to be real soon."

Both are looking flabbergasted. "What the fuck you got going on that you want to stop this plane in midflight?" Nephew asked irked.

"My family. You know. The two ladies that no one ever sees because I'm always out here on some hustle shit. I think it's time that I focus on them for the time being." C answered earnestly.

"I get what you're saying and all. I even understand. But I can't help but think of all the money we're going to be losing if you quit." Nephew selfishly interjected.

"You don't have to worry about losing money. I'm working on my replacement as we speak."

"I know you're not talking about X?" Mr. Lupino asked with disapproval.

"Not at all! He's not ready for the octopus arm. I wouldn't even put him in that type of position. Let's just say I have two separate candidates, and I will be bringing one of them to the table in a week or so. I promise everything will be business as usual. I can't just walk away and let the whole hood starve."

"Well I'm happy for your family, but I can't help but be a little uneasy with the change. You know I don't deal with anyone around here like that and everybody don't know how to keep their lips sealed. I trust you cause I know you were raised to be solid." Mr. Lupino shook his head.

C interrupted. "If you feel any way about the person I send. You don't have to worry about his loose lips. I'll take care of him myself permanently. I promise. But I'm assuring you that I wouldn't be making this type of decision if I hadn't thought it all the way through."

"Look, Bro. I trust you with my life and always have. But you know how we operate, and trust doesn't come easy." Said Nephew.

"I know this is coming out of nowhere to both of ya'll. But I really need to do this. I apologize for any bad feelings ya'll have from this. But I promise my intentions are all good. As a matter of fact, how about I stay down for one more month but keep the person of my choice close to me so ya'll can observe how he moves and if you're not as comfortable as I am promising then I'll stick around a little longer. But if my guy is everything I'm promising him to be then ya'll give me your blessing to live my life. How's that sound?"

Mr. Lupino scratches his head. "It sounds to me like you got your mind made up. I just hope you're not rushing out of this for the wrong reasons and that you're going to regret it later."

"My family can never be a wrong reason. But you guys are my family too. And that's why I feel I have to make sure everything's, everything before I walk away."

"Well, I can't say that I blame you." Nephew said sincerely. "I mean I've been watching you do this since you came home and you're right. I never see your wife and daughter unless we have a cookout. I don't have a ball and chain to worry about. So, with that being said. I can't say I trust you but I don't trust your decision. Go be with your family. Just keep your word cause if your man fucks up and I have to take care of him. It's going to be slow and extremely painful." Sipping his beer. "And in your words… I don't think he's ready for my octopus arm."

"I just don't want us going sideways because I want out. Not counting my aunt and X ya'll pretty much all the family I got outside of my household."

"We're always going to be family. No matter what. With or without business." Mr. Lupino said sternly.

"I really appreciate ya'lls understanding. It really means a lot to me."

Being condescending. "Nobody said we understand. I think you're crazy to be walking away from all this money. But you're a grown man. All I can do is have your back and let life run its course." Nephew held his glass back in the air. "To life."

"To life." C taps glasses again. "Now that we got all the sad shit out the way." C pulls out a big stack of money and lays it on the table. "I ain't out the game yet."

Nephew reached under the bar and grabbed a duffel bag holding five keys of dope. "Two of them have been stepped on and the other three are pure as a virgins pussy."

"Yeah, I'm definitely going to miss this," C says as he studies the keys before placing them back in the bag. "Every time I think you got the best dope money can buy you come with some even better shit."

"Hey, Unc. I know it's not your cup of tea." Refilling their shots. "But do you think me and C can smoke a blunt while we finish chopping it up?

"You boys go ahead. Just make sure you spray good when you're finished. I'm going back upstairs to open the store back up. I'm sure everyone's getting impatient to come in by now."

"I'm going to walk up with you and grab some blunts." C said as he got up from his chair.

"You don't have none on you?" Nephew asked.

"Why bring sand to the beach. I left mine in the car cause I knew I was going to buy some more while I was in here."

"You got some of that to sell? I can smell it from across the room." Nephew stated.

"I got some for sale but not to you. How about I just give you a half?"

"Now you see. You should've said that before telling us you were quitting. The convo could've gone so much smoother."

After C came back with the blunts and began rolling, Nephew says. "I know you're probably tired of talking about it but have you told Bernadette that you're quitting the game?"

"Not yet. I wanted to take her somewhere special and tell her while we were enjoying each other."

"So, where you taking her?"

"I don't know yet. I mean I don't know too many nice places. I'm always in the hood."

"Well, it's a good thing you're talking to me. You should take her to the Poconos."

"I've heard of that place but I don't know what it is."

"Bro. You don't know what you've been missing. It's a vacation resort. But make sure you tell them you want the champagne room."

"What's that? A room full of champagne bottles."

Laughing at C. "Man you are clueless. It's a room with a champagne glass-shaped hot tub. It also has a door that looks like a closet door but it opens up to ya'lls own personal swimming pool." Pulling a business card out of his wallet. "Just call this number and set your reservation. I promise you won't be disappointed.

"You need to call them and demand your commission because I'm sold already." Looking the card over before putting it in his pocket. "I really appreciate this bro."

"I ain't doing this for you. I'm doing it for Bernadette. That lady has been putting up with your shenanigans long enough. She deserves a little pampering."

"I'm about to set this up as soon as I get out of here." Sparking his blunt. "I really am glad life connected me with ya'll."

"Are you going to stop with the bud too? Cause you're the only one that always got killer shit every time."

"Now that, I'm going to leave to X. He doesn't know it but he's been handling about ninety percent of the weed sales already. I only really sell weed to people after the bar. Other than that, I send everyone to X."

"Well, at least I know where to get it from. I can't go without my meds."

Both began to laugh.

CHAPTER 16

Ring, ring, ring. C listens to the phone ring in his ear. "Pick up the phone Bern!" As if she can hear him.

Halfway out of breath when she answers. "Hey, baby! What's up?"

"What the hell you breathing so heavy for? Butt naked man better not be at my house." C said jokingly.

"Boy you know ain't no butt naked man over here. I was running on the treadmill." Looking at herself in the mirror. "Trying to keep my husband's mind right."

"Now you're talking. Where's my princess?"

Looking down the hallway towards Essence's room. "She's in the back playing with her toys. You want me to put her on the phone?"

"Nah. I'm speaking to the person I called for. What you got planned next week?"

"Just my usual everyday activities. Why? What you need me to do?"

"I don't need you to do nothing. What you got planned for the following week?"

"Damn C! What you got going on? I don't have anything planned all month."

"Well, why don't you see if your homegirl wanna come stay a couple of weeks at the house with Essence. Tell her I'll pay her a thousand dollars and I'll leave her some money to take Essence to the movies or something."

"You know she ain't going to say no. But what you got planned?" Trying to sound casual.

"It's a surprise. Just pack up enough clothes to go at least a week and we gonna do some shopping for the rest of the days."

"Well I need to know where we're going, so I know what kind of clothes to pack." Looking into her walk-in closet.

"Just do you. I don't think I've ever seen you not look sexy. Besides if I have my way we ain't going to be wearing clothes most of the time anyway."

"What day do you want me to have her here?"

"You can have her stay over on Sunday because we're going to have to leave out about five in the morning on Monday." Looking over at the paper with all of his vacation information on it and cracking a smile. "I really think you're going to like this."

"Well since you're not going to tell me where we're going. Can I at least ask you what's the occasion?"

"Let's just say the occasion is my wife needs to be reminded periodically that she means more to me than all the crackheads and the dope houses in the world and I just want us to get away from everything and everybody and just enjoy each other like we used to. How's that for an occasion?"

"Now that sounds like just what the Doctor ordered." Putting on her cute voice. "Do you think I can have a little money to grab a couple of things for the trip?"

"Of course, you can. Just get whatever you need out of the box. Oh yeah, I met with Nephew today, so I got to put some things in rotation tonight. So, if you don't see me tonight, I'll be home first thing in the morning. Call me if you need me. I love you Bern."

"I love you too baby. Be careful out there."

"You know I will." They both hang up and C heads straight to the doghouse. Upon entering the house C can hear all the dogs in the house going crazy from hearing the door opening. "Baylo! Baylo! Baylo!" By the third time, he repeats it all the dogs have calmed. C heads upstairs to the room where he keeps his favorite dog. Tapping on the door in a certain rhythm before entering. "What's up Octo!" Seeing his dog wagging his tail in excitement. "What you doing boy?" C petted him all over and slipped his heavy chain off his neck. "This might be our last deposit. Don't worry. I'm always going to have a job for you." Continuing as if

Octo can comprehend. "I just think we've been at it for a long time and it's time for a change. So as soon as this pack runs out, we retire. Deal?" C puts his fist out to be patted by Octo's paw. "My man. I knew you'd be down." C begins to shew Octo away. "Spas, Spas." C moved his bed over and removed a board from the floor exposing a pile of dope. "Got to keep it FIFO. First in first out" C took all the dope out of the hole and put the new dope and returned the other dope on top. C put Octo's bed back over his stash and called him over to him and slid his chain back around his neck. "Watch it. Watch it." C whispered in his ear and dropped a handful of snacks before leaving.

CHAPTER 17

Hearing C's music coming down the street, X steps out the door to hop in the car as soon as he pulls up. "So, what's the occasion you got that we have to go out tonight?"

"My early retirement." Looking down at his watch. "I've come to my final decision. I'm out."

X is taken aback. "I never thought I would ever hear you say those words." Looking around the car through the windows. "Is this a prank show? I know you said you were contemplating the whole idea of quitting. But I thought that was as far as it was going to go."

Correcting X. "Well, you were very wrong. I think there ain't going to be any better time than now. So, we about to go to the bar and drink the past behind us." C drove to the Stallion which was a bar on Main Street where everybody went. As soon as they entered C walked to the bar and addressed the bartender. "What's going on NiNi?" Flipping through his money. "Here is three hundred to start a tab. Let me know when I get down to fifty."

"I can do that but that's not how you run a tab," NiNi said as she laid napkins in front of C and X.

"Well, that's how I'm running a tab. And you keep on trying to make me look dumb in front of my padres I'm going to forget how to run a tip. Now let me get two doubles of gin and two Coronas."

"Look at these niggas," X said to C as he pointed to Tank and Peewee entering the bar.

"Hell got to be freezing over." Peewee yelled out when he noticed X and C at the bar." You two upper echelon ass motherfuckers coming to the pits of the hood to bless us, commoners, with your presence. I got to buy you guys some drinks."

"No! I'm buying the drinks." C said firmly before flagging down the bartender. "Give them whatever they want for the rest of the night on me."

"What ya'll be drinking on tonight? Two doubles of Henny, one Heineken and one Corona Right?" Referring to what they order every night.

"You kn-kn-know how your man gets d-d-down. That's why I love you." Stuttered Tank.

"You don't love me. You just love that I make you the biggest drinks." NiNi responded sassily.

"And you got the sof-softest ass." Tank said as he grabbed a handful.

Smacking him on his arm. "I told you I ain't fucking with you like that no more! I don't know why you can't get the picture."

"I-I-I got the picture. The pi-picture of you on yo-your knees ta-taking this dick."

"Too bad it takes you longer to tell me to take the dick than it does to actually give it to me." Knowing she won with her remark by the cheering she got from everyone, NiNi walks away.

"Man, I got to ge-ge-get me some more of that." Tapping C on the arm. S-so when you gonna quit starving the hood?"

C smiled and held up his shot. "Everything will be up and running before the sun comes up in the morning." Tipping his drink back. "Just hit me as soon as you get up. I'll be ready."

"Aye!" Peewee screeched. "It's about time. The hood without dope is like a clock without arms."

"Word." Agrees Tank. "There goes my ba-baby" Seeing NiNi return with their drinks.

NiNi sets their drinks on the table as well as the bottles she poured them from. "I figured ya'll could use the rest of these bottles. I already made my profit off of both of them." Giving a flirty smile to Tank as she walked away.

"I-I-I knew you loved me."

C pours himself another shot and holds it in the air. "To life. We only get one, so let's do the most with it."

"We will first thing in the morning," Peewee says before taking his shot. "Speaking of one life." Pulling X under his arm and pointing across the bar. "Why you be bullshitting like you don't want to fuck with Aury's fine ass. Ya'll little dudes don't know good pussy when ya'll see it. Let me be young again and I'll show ya'll asses how it's done." Peewee shook his head looking at NiNi's little sister Aury across the bar. "I think she is having ya'll little asses scared."

X quickly correcting Peewee. "First of all. You ain't never going to be young again with your Fred Flintstone looking ass. And secondly, I know the pussy good. I have been hitting that and that's why these other little niggas can't. I have just been falling back because every time we fuck she be on some boyfriend, girlfriend shit and I ain't with all of that."

"With a disgusted look on his face. "Nigga you stupid! She's literally the baddest young chick in the hood hands down and you don't want to lock her down? Don't be crying when one of these lames slide in on your coochie. Shit if you wait long enough and let her turn eighteen it might be me." Winking at Aury across the room. "Don't say I didn't warn you. Once I hit, she ain't never coming back."

C jumps in the conversation. "Man, that nigga don't listen. I have been telling him he needs to lock her down for two summers now. I told him there are three platforms of head niggaship in the hood."

"Head niggaship?" Contested Peewee.

"Yeah, head niggaship. It's like leadership but in the hood. I'm going to need ya'll to catch up on your hood grammar. But like I was saying. There are three types of head niggaship." Counting down on his fingers. "One is the nigga with the most scraps. Everybody fears this guy. Next is the nigga with the most money. Everybody either loves him or hates him. And last is the nigga with the baddest bitch. Which would be you if you weren't so scared." Pointing at X. "Everybody wants to be that nigga."

"Ya'll talking out of the side of ya'lls necks!" Deflects X. "I'm about to go lock her down right now, for no other reason but to prove you wrong." Pointing back at C.

Flabbergasted. "Prove me wrong? How the fuck are you going to prove me wrong?"

Condescending. "You said it's three different head niggas in the hood. But I only heard one." Mocking C, counting down on his fingers. "I got better scraps then anybody my age in the hood. I got more money than anybody my age in the hood. And in about five minutes I'm going to have the baddest chick in the hood than anybody my age." Holding his hand out. "Let me see your keys real quick."

"Don't leave with my car X!"

"I'm not going anywhere. I just want to take her outside." After grabbing the keys X walks up behind Aury and whispers in her ear. "You should step outside with me for a second. I want to talk to you about something."

Aury covers her heart with her hands. "Aww. Look who wants me all to himself."

"You know I always want you all to myself." Turning Aury around to face him, X looks deep in her eyes. "You used to like that about me."

"I used to love that about you until you became Mr. Bigshot around here for all your flunky friends. Now you don't have time for little old me." Batting her eyes.

"That's what I want to talk to you about if you would come outside." X leads the way to the car. As soon as they get in X grabs a blunt from the ashtray and lights it. "For real what I wanted to talk to you about is I think it's time I stop playing around and get myself, somebody, to share my times with. You know, someone that I can trust and depend on, cause we're on the same team."

"So, what? You want me to help you find a girlfriend?" Acting clueless.

Smacking his lips. "You're funny. You know what I'm trying to say. We have been messing around off and on for about two years on some secret shit and everybody knows. I just think its time we stop fooling ourselves and be together. You know how I feel about you and I don't want to see you with nobody else. And you know you don't want to see me with nobody else."

"I don't care who you mess with."

"Stop playing with yourself. You about flipped your wig on me when you thought I was fuckin with Lauren."

"That's just because I don't like Lauren"

"That's just because you don't want me with nobody else." "Leaning in and kissing her. "So, what do you say… You going to be mine?"

"Boy you know I've always been yours. I have been waiting for you to want to be mine." Looking at X sternly. "Don't be playing with me! If you sober up in the morning and realize you did too much, then tell me! Don't have me out here looking stupid!"

"I'm not drunk for one. And the only thing I want to say to you in the morning is roll over so we can do it again."

"You always being nasty." Pecking X on the lips. "You're lucky you're cute"

Noticing people rushing out of the bar in a panic X jumps out of the car. "Fuck! I got to go get C!" Pushing his way through the crowd, X can see Tank and C trying to get at each other. NiNi barely holding Tank back and Peewee holding C trying to talk him calm. "What the fuck is going on?" Grabbing Peewee's arm. "Let me get him! You get Tank!"

With no hesitation, Peewee wraps his arms around Tank and yells. "Let it go, Bro! Let it go!"

Tank infuriated. Shouting without a stutter. "Bitch, ain't nobody scared of you! And the hood doesn't owe you shit! Who the fuck you think I am?"

C inviting the threat. "You know I stay ready bitch! I'm trying to look out for you! But you got to pay your bills like everybody else! You know how I get down! I'll make you famous!"

X gripped his arms around C's body. "Not here cuz! This ain't the time! Let's go!" They hurry outside to the car. "Here's your keys."

Refusing them. "You drive with your sober ass. I'm fucked up!"

"I got it!" Pulling off. "What the fuck happened with ya'll? I swear niggas was just kicking it when I stepped outside."

"Bitch ass nigga thought he was going to get something for nothing. Mad because I won't wipe his bill and I told him he had to pay at least half of it before I fuck with him on any more credit. He started talking greasy to me like I'm some type of punk or something." Looking in his rearview mirror to see what car was behind them. "Turn at this next street." C continued watching to see that no one was following them. "We good. Go to my spot. But stop by the store on the way so we can get some blunts."

CHAPTER 18

X pulled into the gas station. "This guy." He mumbled under his breath, noticing C has fallen asleep. "I wish I had a camera right now." Walking in the store. "What's up Rocky. Let me get two packs of blunts."

"Is that all?" Asked Rocky.

Snapping his fingers. "Damn! I almost forgot something to drink." X went to the back of the store and opened the cooler.

Pop! Pop! Pop! Pop! Shots rang out. "Get the fuck down!" Rocky yelled at X.

As soon as the shooting stopped X jumped up and ran outside. "C! Fuck, C!" Noticing C slumped over in the car soaked with blood. "I got you cuz!" X jumped in the driver seat and noticed Tank's car speeding through the intersection. "I swear I'm going to handle this for you. These niggas are not about to get away with this shit. Just hold on!" Speeding through the traffic lights. "Please hold on!" Hearing C making a gargling noise. "Just keep fighting cuz. We almost there." X honked the horn repeatedly as he pulled under the emergency ramp.

Within seconds there were four nurses at the car rushing to get C into the hospital.

"Hurry up. Please don't let him die!" Panicked X.

One of the male nurses laid his hand on X's shoulder. "You got to trust us. I promise we're going to do whatever we can to save him. But we must get him to surgery now. You might want to take this time to contact any family and let them know what's going on."

After watching them push C to the back, X goes and calls his mother. "Ma somebody shot C! We're at Trumbull! You got to get up here!"

"Oh my God. Is he okay?" Scrambling to get her shoes on. "I'll be there in five minutes. I'm going to call Bernadette and tell her to meet us up there."

Before X could say yes, ma'am Ms. Carol hung up. "Please Lord protect him and don't let him die. I know it's all up to you. We need him." Prayed X, thinking about the amount of blood he saw. "Please Lord I also ask you to bless me with the strength and courage to handle this. Amen."

CHAPTER 19

Standing in the mirror admiring her body in her new outfit. "Damn girl you look so fucking good." Bernadette mocked C's composure. "You about to make me do some things to you." Laughing as she dropped her dress to the floor. "Yup. I still got it." Turning sideways to see all her curves. "Bye-bye flat stomach. Here comes baby belly." The phone rings. "That's probably my baby right there." She fumbled through the clothes she laid on her bed to find her phone and answered without looking. "Hello." In her sweetest voice.

"Bernadette." Ms. Carol's voice paused.

"What is it, Auntie?"

Trying to hold it together. "It's C baby. C's been shot! I need you to get to Trumbull as soon as you can!"

"Oh my God! No!" Bernadette fell back on the bed bellowing. Taking a moment to gather herself. "Is he alive?"

"Yes, he is. But Xavier said it looked bad and they rushed him to surgery. I'm on my way there now. Do you need me to come get you? You probably shouldn't be driving right now."

"No. He needs you there with him. I'm going to be there in no time. Trust and believe me. Please just call me if you hear anything."

"I will. You just drive safe. I can't take anything else happening tonight. I'll see you when you get there."

Bernadette threw on her clothes and ran in Essence's room. "Baby wake up! We got to go!" Seeing her barely responding Bernadette scooped Essence up in her arms like a baby and carried her to the car.

"What's the matter, mommy?" Essence asked as she wakes to her mom crying while buckling her in.

"Something happened to daddy baby. So, we have to hurry up and make sure he's alright." Shaking the seatbelt to check that it's secure. "Aunt Carol and cousin X are with him right now." Jumping in the driver seat and speeding off. "Please God keep him. Please God keep him." Bernadette repeated her prayer the whole fifteen-minute ride to the hospital. "Come grab Essence out the back," Bernadette said to X who has jogged up after seeing her park.

"I got her. Go ahead in. My mom's waiting for you in the lobby." Leaning on the car. "I'll be in with this little pumpkin head in a few minutes. I needed to get out of there and get some air."

"Everything's going to be okay. God got this." Hugging X. "I'll be inside. Make sure she brings her blanket with her when she comes." Making haste through the parked cars Bernadette can see Ms. Carol pacing as soon as she enters the hospital. "What are they saying?"

"Hey, baby." Embracing Bernadette. "They ain't saying nothing at all baby. But God says he's here. I know you been praying. Just keep on praying and this storm is going to get behind us."

"Oh, Lord. That's probably the only reason I'm halfway holding it together. That and I got to be strong for my baby." Squeezing Ms. Carol tighter as tears flooded down her face. "I just told him that my baby been having dreams of him being killed. And he planned a trip for us to get away for a while. Just us." Wiping the tears from her face. "Let me pull myself together before X brings Essence in. I don't want to worry her more than she already is."

"Honey, I understand. Nobody male or without children will ever know how strong you really have to be to be a mother." Guiding her to the couch. "We should probably sit down. It's most likely going to be a few hours before they are done with him."

X came in and laid Essence on the couch across from his mother. "Hey, Bern. Can I talk to you outside for a minute? Leading the way out the door X walks off in the grass away from foot traffic. "I just wanted to let you know what happened."

"You were with him when this happened?"

"I was but I was in the store. All I know is he was sleep in the car when we pulled in the gas station right there on Todd. I went in to grab a couple of things and while I was grabbing some pop out of the cooler shots started flying through the store. I'm on the ground. The store dude on the ground. When the shooting stopped, I got up and ran out to the car where I see C shot up."

"Well do you have any idea who it was?"

"I really don't but the streets are going to talk and I'm going to be right there when they do. I just wanted to tell you that I am going to personally handle this just like I know C would if it were me."

Uneasy. "Please don't go out here trying to be like him. We don't need anything else bad happening."

"I'm good. He taught me everything I know." Giving a wink. "Let me tell my mom I got to go get out of these clothes." Walking back into the hospital. "Hey, mom. I'm going to run to the house and get out of these bloody clothes."

"How are you getting there?" Asked Ms. Carol.

"I have C's car." Dangling C's keys in the air.

"Well take my car. Nobody needs to be driving that car tonight." Handing him her keys. "X. Don't go doing nothing stupid. You hear me?"

"Yes, ma'am I hear you. I'm not going to do anything at all."

CHAPTER 20

After changing clothes X rides slowly past Tank's house observing his car in the driveway. "This shit ain't going to slide. I'll be back motherfucker." Speaking to his self. "Ain't no backing down. Stay right here." Pumping his self-up as he speeds off. Pulling up on the block he spots Timmy standing with a group of guys waiting on sales to come through. "Come here real quick. I got to holla at you."

Timmy hops in smiling but instantly notices the solemnness on X's mug. "What's the deal homie?"

"I'm trying to find Joe Joe. Have you seen him?"

"Shit. I saw that nigga about an hour ago flying through here on a bike. You know Joe Joe. Always on some hot boy shit. It looked like he was heading to his house." Coaxing out the business. "What's up with ya'll two? Ya'll got beef?"

"Nah. Don't say nothing but somebody shot C tonight. I just need to get up with him to see what he might have heard."

"Damn bro! What the fuck is really going on around this bitch?" Reassuring. "You know where I'm at if you need some help putting in some work. I'm going to be out here on the block all night. And I got my thing on me." Lifting his shirt to flash his gun.

"I appreciate you bro, but I'm good. All I need from you is your silence on what we're talking about."

Agreeing with a handshake. "Man, I already forgot what you were saying."

"That's why I fuck with you Bro. You have always been solid since we were stealing penny candy from Giant Eagle."

Laughing at the memory. "We all we got."

"You don't know how much I feel that right now." Seeing Timmy about to exit the car. "Hey! Do you have a blunt on you I can buy? I'll give you five bucks for it." Pulling out his money. I left the ones I bought in C's car."

Dropping a blunt on the passenger seat. "I don't want your money. Just be safe bro."

"Good looks homie." Pulling around the corner to the hood. "Man, I hope this nigga is up in here." Looking up at Joe Joe's window while he knocks on the door.

Joe Joe's mother answers the door. "Look what the cat dragged in" Stepping aside to let him enter. "Your boy is upstairs getting on my fucking nerves." Scratching the sores on her arms. "Tell him I said send me down something small if I'm going to be playing his door bitch all night. Ain't shit for free around this fucking house."

"I'll tell him." X ran up the steps and barged in Joe Joe's room.

Raising his gun to point at X. "What the fuck you think you're doing bro? You trying to die tonight?"

"That's exactly what I need."

"What, one of these hot ones?" Questioned Joe Joe.

"Not quite but I do need some heat. Somebody shot C tonight."

Sitting his gun down, with it still aimed at X. "Stop playing man. Who shot C?"

"Do it look like I'm playing." With tears in his eyes. "That motherfucking stuttering ass nigga Tank." Pounding his fist on the dresser. "He got to go. Tonight! Now! Can I hold a gun or what?"

"You know I got you but what's your plan? You think they just going to let you knock on their door and shoot them back? Nah. We got to figure out a way to get in their spot." Rubbing his chin.

"We?" Queried X.

"Yeah, we!" Exclaimed Joe Joe. "You didn't think I would let my best friend go out here all alone and get his self-killed without me did you? Besides your obviously not thinking straight." Handing his gun to X. "You can roll with this. It's got eighteen shots all together. Seventeen in the clip and one in the head. Be careful you don't shoot yourself."

Examining the gun in his grasp. "I got this. Don't worry about me. But how are you going to roll if I got your gun?" Seeing Joe Joe crawl under his bed. "What the fuck are you doing?"

Joe Joe stands up holding a sawed-off shotgun. "I've been waiting for a reason to break my bitch's virginity." Kissing the barrel of his gun. "You know I stay strapped nigga." Cocking his gun. "Grab that mask off my dresser and I'm going to use my scarf and my hoodie to hide my face."

"Let's do this!"

CHAPTER 21

Bernadette buried her face in C's lap as she cried out. "You got to wake up honey. I need you. Essence needs you. The baby in my stomach needs you. I can't raise this family without you."

Ms. Carol placed her hand on Bernadette's shoulder. "Baby in your stomach? Since when Bern?"

"I went to the Doctors a couple of weeks ago. I was waiting for the right time to tell him. Now I'm scared that I won't get the chance." Sobbing.

"You're going to get the chance. He's going to wake up." Rubbing C's face. "He just needs to rest up for a little bit. He's been through so much tonight." Ms. Carol looked up to see a tall slim gentleman standing in the doorway. "Can we help you?"

The man scans the room before entering. "Carol Jones? Carl's twin?"

"Do I know you?" Weak voiced.

"It's me, Carol. Stoogy!" Pointing at his self. "I used to run with your brother in high school before I left to join the military."

Covering her mouth. "Oh my God! Stoogy! That is, you!" Embracing him. "I didn't recognize you. You got so tall. And you cut your beard and your afro off! So that's what you look like under there. What have you been up to?"

"Well after I served fifteen years in the army I became a police officer in Dayton. After six years I got promoted to detective. And as of last year, I got transferred back here as a detective. And as of an hour ago. I am the lead detective assigned to this case."

"Oh, Lord. You've got to find whoever shot my nephew?" Pleading.

"Is this the same young man who had a run-in with Santose some years back?"

Nodding in agreement. "Yes, he is. My nephew Little Carl and this is his wife Bernadette."

"Nice to meet you." Bernadette offers her hand. "And thank you for taking my husband's case."

Giving a slight smile. "The pleasures all mine. And let's be clear. I didn't take this case. God gave me this case. And as my promise to God and you two. I am going to do whatever it takes to get to the bottom of this. I owe his father my life. And now I finally get to try and even us out." Looking over to Carol. "Besides, I've been dreaming of seeing this lady again."

"You better get out of here." Blushing.

"You know I always had the biggest crush on you. Your brother probably told me a million times that he was going to hurt me about you."

"He was always threatening everybody about me."

"Oh, those weren't threats. Those were promises. And he meant every last one of them." Looking Ms. Carol in the eyes. "Now before I get myself hurt in here can I ask you, ladies, a few questions?"

"I honestly don't know anything about what my husband had going on." Holding her head down. "Or who would want to hurt him."

Ms. Carol interjected. "I'm sorry but neither one of us is going to be any help. But if you could leave me a card or something. I'll give you a call when I get by my son. If anyone knows anything about my nephew's life, it's my son."

"Well here's my card." Handing one to each of them. "I know you feel like you can't be of any help. But if there's anything you can think of as far as even something so slight as someone that might have flipped him the bird in traffic or anything give me a call. And in the meanwhile, we have the shell casings from the scene getting printed. And we're going to run them through the system to see if they tie in with any other cases we have open. We also have the stores surveillance footage getting looked over. We're going to get to the bottom of this."

"I feel so much better knowing someone close to the family is over his case." Rubbing C's arm. "I'm going to step out in the hallway and talk with Stoogy. I mean the detective. I'll be right back." Grabbing her hand. "And remember. He's just resting. He'll be waking up soon."

CHAPTER 22

X parked in the driveway of an abandoned house down the street from Tank's house. Rolling down his window to speak to a fiend he saw coming from Tank's spot. "Hey, Darla. Hop in the back. Let me holla at you real quick."

"Ya'll boys ain't got no homework to do?" Climbing in the back seat. "What ya'll want me to do, tutor ya'll in sex ed?" Rubbing the back of X's head.

"Maybe I'll set you up with my homie later. But for right now I just need a favor." Handing her twenty dollars. "Who all did you see when you were in Tank's crib?"

Stuffing the money in her bra. "I don't know what kind of trouble you're planning. But keep my name out of it. All I saw was Peewee and Tank's bitch ass."

Joe Joe laughing. "Why you don't like Tank?"

"He knows he be cutting up. I be spending all kinds of money with his ass and he acting like he can't serve me a nick. Talking about I better go get some more money and come back."

X pulls out twenty more dollars. "That first twenty was for the information. This twenty is for you to go back down there and buy a rock with."

"And how is that helping you out?" Stuffing that money as well.

"Let me worry about that. You just do what I asked, or you can give me my money back and I'll buy someone else some dope with it."

"No need to jump to conclusions." Opening her door to get out. "I got you, baby boy."

"And you better not tell them that we out here!" Threatened Joe Joe.

"Tell your boy to calm down. It ain't that serious." Walking away.

"So, you think it's a smart idea to have her crack head ass in the mix?" Asked Joe Joe.

"We needed a way to get in the door." Putting his mask on. "There's our way." Watching Darla enter Tanks crack house he jumps out of the car.

"And to think I doubted you. You might be a little gangster after all." Following X through the backyards until they reached Tank's yard. "Stay ducked down. I just saw Peewee walk past the window."

"I-I knew you were ho-ho-holding out." Tank stammered.

"She wasn't holding out. Her trick ass just went and sucked some dick. You know how Darla gets down."

Handing her a rock. "Well whoever di-dick you been sucking. Keep s-sucking it un-until his pockets are empty."

"I'm a hustler. I don't got to suck dick to get my money." Putting the rock under her tongue. "I been out here getting money before ya'll was even allowed to leave your mama's yards."

"Yeah. That's why you got stacks on deck. Huh?" Opening the door to let her out. "Fuck!"

Pow! Pow! Pow! X knocks Peewee off his feet with the shots from his Glock. "C'mon!" Running in the door with Joe Joe on his heels wielding a massive cannon. He runs up on Tank who is reaching for his gun. "Sit your motherfucking ass back down!" Butting Tank in the head with his gun.

Startled. "Ta-take everything. The money i-i-is under the bed. The dope is under the s-sink. Just don't shoot me!"

X removes his mask. "I don't give a fuck about your dope or your money!" Putting his gun to Tank's head. "You didn't think I was going to come for you for shooting C?"

Tank pointed at Joe Joe who was removing his scarf. "This motherfucka…"

Boom! Joe Joe let one off into Tank's chest. Splattering blood all over X. "Come here, bitch." Signaling Darla to kneel down with a wave of his gun.

"I ain't going to say nothing!" Darla screamed in panic.

Boom! Joe Joe pulled the trigger taking off the top half of Darla's head. "She saw our faces, Bro!" Noticing X's astonishment. "We got to go!" Joe Joe ran in the back room and grabbed a lockbox from under the bed and grabbed a bag of dope from under the sink on his way out the door. "Snap out of it! Let's go!" Pulling X by the arm.

After cutting back through the backyards they jump back in the truck. "We killed them niggas!" X shouted as he turned the car on.

"Go through there." Joe Joe directed X to drive straight through the connecting yard, to the next street. "We're going to have to get out of the truck?" Hearing police sirens in the distance. "They're going to be pulling over any car they see coming from this area."

Pulling to the side of the road behind another parked car." Hide everything before we get out." Ducking through the yards on the way to the hood. "I can't believe you shot Darla."

"What the fuck you mean?" Joe Joe disputes. "She saw our faces. And you got her involved."

"I know but she was innocent."

"Ain't no such thing as an innocent crack head. We probably saved her from a lifetime of dying slowly from aids or something."

"And what about Tank? What do you think he was about to say?"

"Probably what everybody says before they get shot. No! Not me! I don't want to die!" In his best pitiful voice. "Look. You did what you were supposed to do. Don't bitch up on me now. If it were you that got shot. C would kill this whole city. And I would help him." Reassuring. "Don't worry. It gets easier over time."

CHAPTER 23

The sun is barely comfortable in the sky when X and Joe Joe go to retrieve his mother's car. "You take the guns and the loot with you." X handed Joe Joe the lockbox they had tucked under the driver seat. "I'm going to go meet up with my mom and Bernadette to see how C is doing."

Feeling the weight of the box. "Boy! It's got to be some racks in here?" Trying to find a place to tuck everything in his clothes. "You take the box with you. I'll take the guns and the dope." Sliding it under the passenger seat. "We can split the money up later when we link up."

"That's a plan." Watching Joe Joe walk away. "Thanks again, Bro. You know, for having my back last night."

"I'm always going to have your back. Now cut the emotional shit before you grow tits." Joe Joe turned and jogged away.

X played last night's incident over and over to himself as he drove home. "What was that nigga trying to say?" Talking under his breath. "Fuck it now. He probably was just trying to talk me out of it. Dumb ass shouldn't jump in the water if he can't swim! Now they done got snatched up by the octopus arm, just like C said they would if they crossed him." Justifying what he did. "Damn, it looks like they're up in here." Noticing his mom's front door open when he pulls up. "It's smelling good in here!" X walked up and hugged his mom who was at the stove cooking. "You sure know how to brighten a new day. How's C?"

"Well besides the tubes and the I.V.s looking so uncomfortable. The doctor says everything's stable. He still can't talk yet, but before we left, he would squeeze our hands to let us know he could understand." Looking over at Bernadette who is asleep on the couch. "Wake that poor child up so we can eat and get back up to the hospital."

"What time did ya'll come to the house?" Inquired X.

Looking up as if she could see the time in the air. "I think it was around seven when we left. The doctor said when we get back up there, C should be in his own room and out of the recovery area. I just figured it was a good time for her to rest and get some nourishment. Lord knows she needs it."

"Where's Essence?"

"Oh. One of Bern's friends came by and picked her up right after you left. She's going to keep her so Bern can be at the hospital with C."

Bernadette's body jolted when X shook her. "I'm so sorry. My mom told me to wake you so you can eat."

"It's not your fault." Sitting up on the couch. "All this drama got me all over the place. How are you holding up?"

Letting out a chuckle. "I'm dealing with it."

"You better not have done nothing stupid Xavier." Ms. Carol snapped.

"I didn't do nothing. Besides, I don't know who shot C even if I wanted to do something. Who am I supposed to do something too?"

"I'm just worried about you baby. I know your hurting. But more violence ain't going to make things better."

"I know mom. But can I use your car for a little bit longer? I want to get dressed and pick up Aury to come to the hospital with me."

"I don't mind. Just make sure you get up there early. C really needs you there." Smiling. "And I know you don't like me calling her your girlfriend, but I really do like that girl."

Scarfing down her breakfast. "I tell him that every time he brings her to my house. They remind me of me and C before Essence."

"Well, I would have you two to know." Rubbing his hands together. "That as of last night. Me and Aury are now really a couple."

"At least that's some good news." Ms. Carol stated. "Well seeing how Bern is crucifying that plate I'm going to assume that we're about to run out the door in a few seconds. I'm going to grab my stuff quickly so I can be ready."

Watching to make sure Ms. Carol was out of sight Bernadette pulled an envelope out of her purse and handed it to X. "C told me if anything was to ever happen to him, that I was to give this to you." Peeking down the hall. "Tuck it somewhere and open it when we leave."

"I got you." Slipping the envelope under the couch cushion.

Walking back in holding a gym bag. "Oh, yeah. I'm going to have the detective come over in a few minutes and ask you about last night."

"A detective? Why does he need to talk to me?"

"Because you're the only one that knows anything about C's life out here." Ms. Carol said sternly.

"And I know that no detective needs to know what he got going on out here." X looking grim.

Bernadette cuts in. "You're a smart boy. And I'm going to need you to talk to this man if you think you might know something to help him find who shot my husband. You don't have to say anything that you think might harm him. But talk to him."

Ms. Carol fighting her tears. "This is a good man, the detective. And he was a good friend to your uncle. There's a reason outside of what we have the power to know or control that this man got this case. I feel it in my spirit that this is for our good."

"I'll talk to him. Just give me like twenty minutes to get dressed before you send him around here."

As soon as they pulled out of the driveway X tore the envelope open. "This nigga always got a plan." Pulling out a letter with two keys taped to it. "Man be strong." Pumping himself to read the letter. After reading it he folds it and stuffs it under his bed and proceeds to get dressed.

Moments later. Knock! Knock! Knock! "Detective Patterson. I'm looking for Xavier." The officer states through the door.

"Here I come." X sprayed a squirt of air freshener in the air before answering the door. "Hey. You can step in and talk." Shaking his hand as he entered. "My mom said you had some questions for me?"

"Yes. And first of all. I'm sorry about what happened to your cousin. And I don't care about anything he might do to get money. All I'm concerned with is who shot him." Crossing his arms. "Now you were the last person with him before he got shot. And you were the first person to see him after he got shot."

"Like I told my mom. When we pulled into the gas station C was sleep. I went in the store back by the coolers and that's when the shooting started. I dropped to the ground for cover and when the shots stopped, I ran outside to find my cousin shot up. End of story."

"Do you know two guys known by the names Tank and Peewee?"

"Yeah why? What about them?" Trying not to look nervous.

"They were shot last night as well and we don't know if it could have been connected. When was the last time you seen them?" The detective interrogated X.

"Last night at the bar," X said.

"Yeah. And I heard at that bar that they had some type of altercation."

"I mean they exchanged words. Nothing that I would call an altercation." Displaying his frustration. "They always go back and forth like that. Then they both sober up. Then they go right along like nothing ever happened."

"So where were you last night after you left the hospital?"

"I came here and changed out of my clothes and then I went to my girlfriends for the rest of the night."

"Well, I'm just going to be frank with you. Whatever is going on out here seems like it's just the beginning. So, if I were you, I would stay clear from the bullshit. At the same time if you can think of any detail no matter how small. Give me a call." Handing X a card. "I'm here to help." While walking out they see

Joe Joe and Timmy approaching. "Be careful out there. I'll be in touch."

"What the fuck did he want?" Joe Joe barks watching the detective pull off.

"He wanted to know if I saw anything last night when C got shot."

"What did you say?" Asked Joe Joe.

"What you mean what I say? I said I didn't see shit. Because I didn't see shit." Raising his tone.

"I don't like that motherfucker. He's the officer that ran up after we was shooting out in the projects. I told you I dove on the ground with the kids like I didn't have nothing to do with it and he ran right past me. After I saw him bend the corner, I got ghost. I swear he been watching me ever since."

"Yeah that shit was crazy. I'm the one that told you they were coming." Timmy said proudly.

"Yeah. That's one time you did right. He was there so fast though." Joe Joe recollected that day. "You would've thought we got set up."

"Oh shit!" X acted like he just remembered. "He also said somebody smoked Tank and Peewee last night." Giving an eye to Joe Joe. "He said they think the shootings might be connected."

"Man, fuck what he's talking about. Let him do his job and figure something out. The streets are going to talk though. And when they say who shot C, we ain't waiting on no police to handle it for us." Giving X the eye back with Timmy unaware.

"You're right. Fuck what he's talking about. I got a proposition for ya'll if you're interested." X said, diverting the attention.

"You already know I'm down." Remarked Timmy.

"What kind of proposition?" Inquired Joe Joe.

"Well with C getting shot. I have to get rid of the dope. So being that ya'll sell more dope than most older niggas I know. I want to front it to ya'll at a killer price that ya'll can even sell weight if you want." X selling the deal.

"And what about the octopus arm?" Asked Joe Joe.

"My octopus arm ain't that high so it ain't as hard to reach as C's." Knowing he had him. "I'm going to pick ya'll up later and we're going to put something together."

Timmy looking unsettled. "Man fuck! I have to keep my little brother tonight. Can I still get the same deal tomorrow?"

X feeling his self. "You can get that deal today, tomorrow, or next week. Just let me know when you're ready." Directing towards Joe Joe. "You down with tonight?"

"I'm waiting for you!" Jokes Joe Joe. "But while we're waiting let's smoke before you got to start handling business." Holding a blunt in the air.

"Let's step out back."

CHAPTER 24

"Look who's here to see you," Bernadette says, rubbing C's head. "He can't talk but if you let him hold your hand he can squeeze once for yes and twice for no." Raising out of her chair. "You can sit on this side where he can see you better."

"How you been Bernadette?" Aury's soft voice came from behind X. "I'm so sorry for everything you're going through." Hugging Bernadette.

"Where's my mom at?" X asked curiously.

"She said she was going to the cafeteria." Looking up at the clock. "I thought she would be back by now." Grabbing Aury's hand. "So, I heard through the grapevine that a certain unnamed couple has decided to go exclusive." Winking at X.

"Do you hear your wife?" X says to C jokingly. "Oh shit! He just squeezed my hand!"

"I told you that's his way of answering you. Once for yes and twice for no."

"C. We all love you and hope that you get better."

X says proudly. "Yeah, you can't see her over there but that's my girl Aury." Leaning in to whisper in C's ear. "Do you remember last night?"

C confirmed with a squeeze.

"Let's just say niggas got the octopus arm last night so you can focus on getting better."

C began squeezing his hand repeatedly.

Looking up at Bernadette and Aury. "Not to be rude but can ya'll step out for two seconds?"

"Damn! You're kicking me out of my own husband's room?"

"I ain't kicking you out. I'm requesting that you kick yourselves out." Feeling C squeeze his hand firmly. "By C's squeeze, he agrees with me."

"You're lucky me and Aury got some catching up to do." Intertwining her arm with Aury's "Let's blow this popsicle stand."

After seeing the door close. X began to whisper to C again. "Me and Joe Joe touched Peewee and Tank last night. When I came out of the store, I saw them mashing through the light like they were going to get away. I swear I lost it. After I got you to the hospital all I could think about was killing them niggas." Tears began flooding down his cheeks. "I really just went to Joe Joe to grab a gun because I didn't think it would be smart to go to the spot after what happened with you. He was so hell-bent on going with me that I had to take him. I know ya'll don't be seeing eye to eye, but that nigga notched his belt for you last night. With that being said, I want to put him on to help me while you're down. Your letter said to throw the work to Peewee and Tank but now that's impossible seeing that they're no longer with us." Feeling one squeeze. "I won't let you down. I'm going to slide by the doghouse when I leave here and feed them for you." He sat there in silence for minutes just watching C rest.

The door swings open. "Look who we ran into downstairs," Bernadette said walking in the room with Aury and Joe Joe.

"I had my aunt drop me off and I'm going to ride with you if that's cool?" Joe Joe informed X.

Laughing at his approach. "I guess it's got to be. I mean you're here now. We're about to head out anyways." X patted C's chest and turned to hug Bernadette. "Tell my mom I'll be back up here to pick her up in a little bit."

"Don't worry about it. I'll take her home when she gets ready. You just be safe out there."

"I will. I'm about to go and feed the dogs."

"Thank you. I didn't even think about those crazy things. If it weren't for you they would probably starve to death." Looking towards Aury. "Speaking of taking care of dogs. Remember what I told you."

"See you think you're funny. This is going to be ya'lls last time talking. I can't have you feeling her head up with your craziness." X said walking out to the hall.

Yelling out the room to him. "Shut up silly and just thank me later." Bernadette took C's hand and whispered to him. "Is everything alright with that boy." Feeling one squeeze. "Thank you, Lord."

Upon entering the doghouse X chanted to calm the barking dogs. "I'm going to need you to carry the food while I carry the water so we can hurry up and get out of here."

"No problem. Just don't let one of these motherfuckers bite me." Joe Joe demanded.

"You good." They walked through the house feeding all of the dogs and when they got to Octo's room X knocked on the door with a rhythm before opening it. "This is C's favorite dog." Motioning Joe Joe to wait outside the door X went in and petted Octo. "You can come in now. You should let him smell you so he knows you."

Joe Joe confused. "Why didn't you do that with the other dogs?"

"This is the dog you need to know. All the other dogs follow him. Trust me." Watching Joe Joe draw closer with his hand extended towards Octo. "Be nice Octo. He's a friend." While Joe Joe petted Octo, X retrieved the dope out of the floor." Damn! I didn't know it was this much. I'm going to have to weigh out a pack for you after I pick up my scale. He doesn't got nothing broke down yet."

Observing the keys of dope X was stashing in the floor. "You might as well just give me a whole key."

"I can't. C gave me strict instructions on how to break it up. I'm going to give you an ounce and you just bring me back eight hundred."

Rubbing his hands together. "Hell yeah! I can fuck with that. I need that tonight!"

After covering it back up X whispered in Octo's ear. "Watch it. Watch it." Then he walks outside and they feed the rest of the dogs.

When they get back in the car X turns to Joe Joe. "I'm going to drop you off, then I'm going to take Aury to get something to eat. After that, I'm going to put that together for you and Timmy.

"Aye aye, captain." Saluting X.

CHAPTER 25

X is in his room weighing out ounces of dope when he hears his mother's voice talking to a man in the living room. "Ma who just came in with you?"

"It's just Detective Patterson. He was just stopping by to check on us." Ms. Carol replied back. "You should come out here and speak."

Tucking the weighed-out ounces in his backpack before stuffing the rest of the dope at the bottom of his hamper. "Here I come ma." As he enters the living room. "What's up again detective?"

"Not much at this moment but I have found a link between the shootings."

Feeling butterflies in his stomach. "Oh yeah? What's that?"

Pointing at the couch. "Do you mind if I sit down."

"Oh no. Go ahead and have a seat. Let me move this blanket for you." Folding the blanket and sitting it on the other side of the couch. "My niece took a nap on here earlier and we kind of left out in a rush."

"Well let me start off by saying whatever I say to you cannot be repeated to anyone."

X making a motion to zip his lips. "My lips are sealed."

"I'm only trusting you because of who your uncle Carl was and is to me. So." Taking a deep breath. "We don't have anything concrete from the ballistics office yet. But without even running the ballistics I can tell you that not only were the shell casings the same caliber but they were also the same brand at both shootings. This leads me to believe they were from the same box of bullets. Meaning whoever shot C shot Tank and Peewee. I'm just hoping the prints lead us to who that person is."

"Totally baffled." Why do you think they were from the same box?"

Cocky. "I'm a good detective. Besides they both share the same markings."

"Man! This is crazy! Who would want to kill all three of them?" Trying to be convincing that it wasn't himself.

"That's exactly what I plan on finding out."

"Well not to be short with you, but I have to go and meet my girlfriend in about fifteen minutes." Excusing himself self from the house. X pulled out of the driveway and sped to the hood. Spotting Timmy immediately. "Yo! Come hop in!"

Timmy jumped in the car. "I thought you was going to get up with me tomorrow?"

"I was actually coming out here to get with Joe Joe and just so happened to see you." Handing Timmy one of the ounces out of his bag. "But since you're still out here. You might as well take this with you." Tucking the bag back behind his seat. "Have you seen Joe Joe's fidgety ass around here?"

"Shit. I saw him like an hour ago. He said he was going to get some pussy. That nigga was probably lying." Getting back out the car. "I'm about to take this in the house right now. What you want back off of it?

"Just bring me eight hundred. If you see Joe Joe tell him I was looking for him." Heading back towards the doghouse. "How the fuck didn't I see this shit? This nigga had me thinking he had my back this whole time." Thinking about last night when everything went down. "That's probably what he was going to say. That he saw Joe Joe shoot C. I'm so fucking stupid." Still running thoughts through his head. "That's why he was pointing that fucking gun at me!" When X pulled up to the doghouse, he could hear the dogs barking frantically. Running to the back to see what was going on X sees Joe Joe running out of the back door.

"Fuck! How the fuck did you get loose?" Joe Joe yelled, noticing Octo was on his heels. As soon as he crossed the tree line to the woods. "Ahh!" He fell from a bite to the leg from Octo. "Get the fuck off of me!" Kicking and screaming to get free from Octo's shaking grip. He pulls his gun from his waist.

"Oww, Oww!" Dropping the gun as Octo sinks his teeth into his arm.

X runs up on Joe Joe being attacked. "Baylo, Baylo." Watching Octo release his grip. "You shot C and now you're trying to rob us." Crouching down to pick up Joe Joe's gun. "You had me kill Peewee and Tank for nothing!" Pointing the gun at Joe Joe.

Joe Joe squirmed backward until he had his back against a tree. Putting his hand up to signal X to stop. "I did everything for me and you. All these niggas have been in our way. C wasn't ever going to let you shine!"

Pow! X put the gun to the side of Joe Joe's head and pulled the trigger. "You were right about one thing." Staring at Joe Joe's dead body. "It did get easier." Wiping the gun off with his shirt before dropping it on Joe Joe's lap and picking up the bag of dope. "C'mon. Let's get you back in the house." Jogging back with Octo chasing behind him dragging his long heavy chain.

CHAPTER 26

X walks into the hospital room to see C standing with his walker and his nurse standing behind him. "I say let him fall. How else is he going to learn?"

"That's because you're an asshole." C said in a weak voice.

"I see your throat is still sore from the tubes."

Bernadette comes out of the bathroom. "They just took the tubes out yesterday. It's going to take at least a week for his throat to feel normal again." Her hand on her hip. "I mean he had them things down his throat for two weeks. I think he's doing good just talking." Giving C a kiss. "Ain't that right baby?"

"You know you're always right." Signaling to the nurse. "I think I've had enough exercise for today." Sitting down slowly. "Man, I can't wait for the pain to stop."

"The drugs they giving you aren't strong enough?" X asked concerned.

"I wouldn't say that. I just think the pain is that bad that it doesn't matter how many pills I take."

The door swings open and in comes Ms. Carol and Detective Patterson. "How's everybody doing this morning?" Greeted Ms. Carol.

"Why do I keep seeing ya'll two together? Is there something I need to know?" Grilled X.

"Now I'm not going to lie to you. I am and have always been crazy about your mom. And if she would let me, I would try to make her the happiest woman on Earth. But until then we are just friends." Reasoned Detective Patterson.

"I knew it was something more than just C's case that's been keeping you around so much." X joked.

"Speaking of C's case. The bullets from C's and Peewee and Tanks' shootings were a match. The bullets from Joe Joe's suicide was also a match. So, with that being said. I closed the case this morning naming Joe Joe the shooter. I just wonder what he was doing way out there in the woods and what attacked him so bad that he shot his own self." Throwing his hands in the air. "Well I guess with Joe Joe dead, all we have are assumptions."

"I still can't believe that Joe Joe did all of this," X stated in denial.

"I can believe it. I always told you that was his character. But you had so much faith in him anyway." Convicted C.

"Well, life paid him back for everything in the end." Ms. Carol interjected "And you're still with us. So, I really think nothing else you guys are talking about matters."

"Oh yeah, and I almost forgot." Directing towards Ms. Carol. "Do you remember where I told you I first saw that boy and later I felt he had something to do with it?"

"Are you referring to that murder in the Highland homes last year?"

"Yes, I am. The same one I saw him at and thought he was just one of the kids. It was just something about the way he was staring at me that made me always question that day. Well, the bullets also matched that shooting."

"Well, I'm just glad that you got this case and you worked it so diligently," Bernadette added.

"I'm happy I could do this not just for him but for his father as well. I'm not going to keep ya'll. I really just came by here today to give ya'll the news." Shaking everyone's hands. "I hope to see you later?" Hinting to Ms. Carol.

"Can all of ya step out so I can have a word with X?" After everyone exits. "So how are you dealing with everything?"

"Pretty good. I just keep remembering what you told me. And even though Tank and Peewee didn't deserve it. I know I did what I did for a real reason. But you were right. It does bother you more afterward." Getting a thought. "Man, I've been meaning to ask you something. What the fuck did you have Octo chained to? Because when I took him back in the house, I couldn't find any sign that he broke free from anywhere."

Cracking up before answering. "He was never chained to anything. I taught him to attack anyone that takes my dope without doing the proper knock or saying those magic words. That's why I stressed you to do everything step by step in that letter. He was only chained up in his mind." Admiring his cousin. "I still can't believe you been out here on so much gangster shit. You've really been handling yourself like a boss. I really am proud of you. And I'm sorry about your friend."

"Evidently he wasn't no friend of mine. And that's exactly why he had to get the octopus arm."

"I couldn't have said that better myself." Agrees C.

ACKNOWLEDGMENTS

This book is dedicated to my mother Josetta Logan. Who always taught me to never be afraid to try. And that God made us all to succeed. Our only failure comes from a lack of belief in who and what we are.

Follow:

Instagram: @visualwording

E-mail: glogantheauthor@gmail.com

2nd Edition

www.ingramcontent.com/pod-product-compliance
Lightning Source LLC
Chambersburg PA
CBHW071404170626
46811CB00003B/1253